LOOK AT YOU

Black Rock
A Kind of Eden
Fortune

AMANDA SMYTH

LOOK AT YOU

PEEPAL TREE

First published in Great Britain in 2025
Peepal Tree Press Ltd
17 King's Avenue
Leeds LS6 1QS
UK

ISBN 13: 9781845235895

Supported using public funding by
ARTS COUNCIL
ENGLAND

CONTENTS

PROLOGUE

I am looking at my father. We are in Trinidad. His blond hair is cut short, and there's no trace of a beard. His eyes are closed, and he is lying very straight and stiff on the pale sand. He could in fact be dead. Only you wouldn't expect a man, tanned, and so young to be dead.

"Look at you," Luke says, and points to a tiny child kicking at the edge of the clear water. Luke isn't there, but he is there in the next photograph. He is young and staring up at a white sky; snow is falling. He is wearing a party hat and holding something, but it is difficult to see what this is. I can make out a blurry shape, and then I remember that it's a remote-control plane. Something is written on the back of the photograph. I read aloud, "Christmas 1972." Luke says "Jesus," and looks hard at the picture.

I push my hand into the bottom of the cardboard box and find my father standing outside the Town Hall in Leeds. His hand is raised as though he did not want to have a photograph taken. He is wearing a knitted cap and a sweater with patches on the sleeves. It's hard to tell exactly how old he is because of his beard. This photograph was definitely taken after my mother had left him. "You'd never know it was the same man," I say to Luke, holding up the photo taken of him in Trinidad. He leans over and examines the two images, and then shakes his head.

In a square snap, my Trinidadian grandparents are perched on a bench, and, to one side, miraculously reflected in a shimmering lake, are the silver pipes of the refinery and a lilac flame shooting out into the bright blue sky. On the left, Helena is in uniform and standing beside a pram. I wonder who is in it and if it could be my mother. And if it is, I wonder if there is a little seed called a "donkey eye", which they say brings luck to a baby, hidden under her pillow. My mother says she never had much luck, but I don't think that's true.

There's Alan, my mother's boyfriend. I can never imagine him young, and why should I. My memories of Alan are exactly like this photograph: a tall, broad man with grey hair and big hands. He is standing outside his house, leaning up against the gate. I know it is winter because the trees are bare. I wonder who took the photograph, and guess that it might have been my mother; he has a particular, tender look.

Here is my father again. This time sitting on the doorstep of his back-to-back house in Leeds. The sun is pouring down on to his face, and the tilted face of his second wife who is cradling a tiny baby, my half-brother. They look very happy. In the background, an older woman is waving at the camera. Shadows from washing lines stretch across the street, and I remember that the house where my father lived didn't have a bathroom.

Next, Alan and me are sitting in a restaurant. I am wearing a white dress, and I am young, twenty-one, perhaps. I also look awkward. Alan has his arm around my shoulder, and he is very thin. "My God," I say, "that was taken just before he died, at The Ivy," and I give the picture to Luke, who passes me a photograph of him, me and Roxy sitting on the fuselage of an aeroplane. An image so clear it might be a postcard. On the back, I recognise the name of a photographer's studio in San Fernando. I think of how many times I have flown across the Atlantic. And how I will probably continue to do so for the rest of my life.

Now, my mother and father are together in black and white on a grassy bank at a place I recognise at once. In the background there is an abandoned car and I can just make out the rough sea. The wind is pushing down the grass and blowing out my mother's hair. She has her arms around my father's neck, and she is staring right into his eyes. I have never seen my mother look at anyone in this way. I would call that love. But my father, he seems to be leaning backwards, and with a dark almost comical expression, pulling away from her, as if he knows something she doesn't know. My mother must be seventeen years old and therefore not yet my mother. I look at this photograph for a long time.

ANN

I liked to watch her face breaking through the surface in the pool, the big blue pool at the club where I played every day during summer holidays. Helena, my grandmother's housekeeper, sat beneath the coloured parasol, while I swam with Luke, and the other children who lived on the refinery camp: swam, and ran about on the hot concrete, and threw coins in the water and dived down to find them, and jumped from the tall diving board.

From there I could see the refinery, the burning lilac flame. I could see the dark green places full of clumps of bamboo. I could see the shimmering lake and the brown bank where vultures made a black crowd. Before we hit the water, we yelled out our names or the name of someone famous who we'd like to be. Sometimes we screamed because the diving board was a skyscraper and the pool below a faraway city. Helena would look up from her bible and say, "Stop that noise, be quiet." And we'd stop for a while, but then someone would throw a coin into the pool, or push someone in, and we'd start shouting again. This would go on all day, until we were told to come in for lunch, or it was time to go home. By afternoon, my skin was wrinkled like an old person's.

I knew Ann was older, by at least three years. Mostly, she sat, in her orange bikini, in a wrought-iron chair, her legs propped on another chair, reading a book. Sometimes, she walked to the edge of the pool, made a steeple with her hands and dived in. Or she swam to the other side, or to the other side and back again. But she never stayed in the pool for long. If we were playing in the deep end, she swam in the shallow. And if we were playing in the shallow end, she swam where the water was deep.

Her name was Ann Sanchez. I would never have spoken to her if I hadn't found her necklace. I was looking for a ten-cent piece when I saw it lying on the grate at the bottom of the pool. I knew it didn't belong to any of us. When I held it up, it sparkled in the sun. Someone said I should keep it. I didn't know what to do. Luke thought I should ask Helena or take it home and ask our mother.

Then I saw her standing by her chair. One hand made a shade over her eyes, the other held on to her hip. Her skin shone like liquorish.

"Hold on a minute," I said to the others, and climbed out of the water. She wrapped a towel around her waist and walked towards me. When I asked if the chain was hers, she looked in the cup of my hand and cocked her head like a bird.

"I've been looking for that for the longest while."

Her voice was soft, tinkling and gentle, like the voice of a stream if a stream could speak. When I dropped the chain into her hand, her full mouth grew wide in a smile, and I thought how large her teeth were. I was about to go back to the shallow end when she asked where I was from.

When I told my mother I had met a girl called Ann at the pool, she asked, as they always ask in Trinidad, if I knew the family name. Sanchez, I said. My mother and grandmother spent the whole evening talking about the Sanchez family they had known when my mother was a child.

So I heard about Mona with the Coca-Cola figure who won a competition for the most beautiful girl in South Trinidad. I heard about Mona's uncle, a teacher who never got married. I heard about her father, who was killed in an automobile accident, and how her mother tried to kill herself by hanging from a light fitting, but someone heard the chair fall, and the rope broke because it was old and frayed. I heard about her mother's lover who lived in Barbados and how he took all her money and threw it away in running a failed fast-food restaurant. This is what happens in Trinidad. You say one name and, next thing, they're talking about the family for hours.

Everyday while the other children played, I sat with Ann. We talked about all sorts of things: music, fashion and film stars. Sometimes I talked about Ireland. I talked about the town where we lived and the rainy beach with coppery rocks. I told her about my father and how he couldn't come to Trinidad because he was starting a new job in a textile company, and that he played drums in a jazz band. Ann said music was good for the soul. She could play the piano up to Grade 4.

She had never had a boyfriend and didn't want to get married until she was at least twenty-five. Her older sisters lived with her mother in London, and they were already talking about getting engaged. She had been to England three times and hoped one day to study music at the Royal College of Music in London. She wanted to compose music for musicals and films. When she talked about this, she moved her hands a lot and her words came in a rushing, energetic way. She liked reading novels, too, novels by Charlotte and Emily Bronte. When she said she wanted to walk on the English moors, walk and walk until it was so dark you couldn't see anymore, I said, it's much too cold. Ann said she couldn't care less if it snowed.

Sometimes we sat on the steps and dangled our legs in the water, or we lay on towels by the side of the pool. We lay on our fronts and faced each other so our words fluttered over the grass. Or we lay on our backs with our arms by our sides and our words went up and seemed to get stuck in the thick, hot air. Sometimes we kept our eyes closed and didn't talk at all.

Ann went home for lunch, but every now and then, when her stepmother, Rosa, was away, and her father, Dr Sanchez, was working at the hospital in Port of Spain, she stayed at the club. Helena said it was okay to go up to the snack bar with Ann. We ordered hamburgers or hot dogs and fries and sweet drinks and brought them back to the table and ate them under our parasol.

One day, we were lying by the pool and Luke was sitting on the diving board eating an ice cream. Ann said she didn't like ice cream but she liked chocolate, especially English chocolate.

I said, "Maybe I can send you some when I go back."

Ann opened her eyes.

"I can put them in one of those special padded envelopes. Mars bars, or Milky Ways, Galaxy, whatever you like."

Ann sat up, and her back made a curve like a bow. She said, "When are you going back?"

I said I wasn't sure but probably sometime soon. I said it in a casual way.

Ann walked to the edge of the pool and dived in. I watched her shape glide through the water to the other side and thought of an arrow passing through air. Then I thought how quickly the summer had passed and how, if I could only wind it back like a movie, I would wind it back to when we met.

That day we went home early. Over lunch, Luke and I listened to my mother and grandmother talk about all the things we had to do before we left. The guava jelly, pepper sauce and pastels had to be made. We had to visit relatives in the city and drive east to see the old house and take pictures of it before it fell down. We had to see the dressmaker, the dentist, a dying aunt I'd never met. There was so much to do. Luke rolled his eyes, and I knew, that like me, he didn't want to do any of those things.

Suddenly Helena was clearing the table, and my grandfather was going to rest. I was thinking about the book I had borrowed from Ann, and wondering if I should read in the verandah or beneath the mosquito net, when my grandmother said, "Why don't you invite her for tea?"

"Who?"

"The Sanchez girl," she said, as though to say, who else could it be? "The Sanchez girl you see at the pool."

So, I rang Ann from the old black phone in the hallway. I said, "Listen, why don't you come for tea?" And she laughed because she was going to call and ask if I wanted to come and have supper at her house. She was going to call, but thought that maybe she should leave it until later, because all now we might be having a rest and she didn't want to disturb us.

"Ann," I said, "you come here because they would all love to meet you. I've been talking about you so much; they can't wait to meet you. It's Ann this and Ann that. And they want to know about your family!"

So, she said yes, but not yes in a way that was polite; she said yes as though it was the most important thing in her whole life.

I was hanging around the kitchen waiting to lick the bowl from the sponge cake when my grandfather came home. He said something about the lazy men on the refinery and how they were only good for two things: making love and dancing. My grandmother made a sshhh sound and put her finger to her lips. In the back room, Helena cleared her throat. I wondered what she thought when she heard him talking like that. I wondered if she hated him, and that, if she did, maybe he should be careful, because Helena knew things my mother and my grandmother didn't know.

Sometimes, when the sky was red, as if the sun had been bleeding, we walked by the long grass and the shimmering lake and Helena told me stories about a terrible woman with a hoof for a foot, and how she took away your soul while you slept. If she took away your soul you might have to spend your whole life looking for it.

"This what make some people restless," she said. "They looking for their soul."

I asked her if that's what made Grandpa that way; that maybe he was trying to find his soul. Helena said no, and then she looked at me in a way I will never forget.

"No, miss," she said. "Your grandpa never had a soul, so how anybody could anybody steal it?"

Luke said Helena was trying to frighten me and I thought he might be right. But I also knew that even if she was, it didn't mean that she was lying.

When the cake was cool, my grandmother covered it with chocolate buttery icing. Then she made a jug of lime-juice from the limes I'd collected in the yard that morning. My mother filled bread rolls with ham and cheese, and there were little pies with mince inside, arranged on a tray. In the dining room, Helena dressed the table with a crocheted cloth and placed a thick group of lilies in a white vase. Above, the old fan was spinning and making its familiar, humming sound. I wondered if Luke was playing cricket in the yard next door. I could hear voices.

I pulled back the net curtain and looked out at the yard where the light was pale gold and thought how lucky I was to have Ann coming for tea. Who knew, maybe we would write to each other for a long time. Maybe she would come and visit me in Ireland! I imagined her in a winter coat, a knitted hat and boots, the two of us lying on a mountain of heather looking up at the Irish sky. And I thought how lucky I was to have a grandfather who sent me a ticket every year, so I could come to Trinidad and make new friends like Ann Sanchez. I felt annoyed with Helena for saying what she said.

*

I sang while I bathed. Then I dressed in my favourite purple top and matching shorts. I combed my long hair and decided to leave it loose. When I first arrived, I was so pale I could trace all my veins like rivers on a map. Now I was a dark reddish brown and the whites of my eyes were like the whites of eggs cooked in a pan. Ann said my eyes were the prettiest eyes she'd ever seen.

"No, Ann, yours are the prettiest," I'd said. "They remind me of night."

I heard the car in the driveway. Then my mother called to say, *Someone's here!* Running down the stairs, my Trinidad slippers made a loud clacking sound. In the kitchen my mother was shaving ice, and my grandmother was sprinkling hundreds and thousands over the cake.

"Take your time, take your time!" my grandmother said.

I ran out, and into the yard and up to the top of the driveway where Ann was waiting. She looked different. She was wearing a white frilly dress and white stockings, and her shoes were shiny with buckles, like shoes I might wear in England. Her hair was parted and bunched with coloured bobbles. She looked younger, too; and her skin seemed smoother and darker in the fading light.

We walked around the front of the house. I showed Ann the swing my grandfather had made, and the cuckoo nest with the tiny eggs. Then I took her into the verandah, where she admired my grandmother's plants and the marble table my uncle had brought from Argentina. Climbing into the green, striped hammock, I noticed her flowery scent.

From this low place, I could see the clear sky and the tops of the coconut trees at the far side. Their fronds were moving like fingers, playing in the silvery light.

"Do you ever wish you could be somewhere else?" Ann said.

"Not right now. I'm happy here with you."

"You're lucky to have two worlds," she said and I didn't quite understand what she meant.

I didn't hear my mother come into the verandah, but when I looked up she was there. I knew at once there was something wrong; and I wondered if she was annoyed that I hadn't brought Ann inside to meet her. Or perhaps she was annoyed that we were both in the hammock at the same time. She always said the hammock couldn't take the weight of two people.

"This is Ann," I said, pointing at my friend, who, with her arms all loose and her stockinged legs flopping over the side of the hammock, must have looked like a cloth doll.

"Hello, Ann."

"It's a pleasure to meet you," Ann said in a polite voice.

"I know we shouldn't both be in the hammock at the same time," I said, struggling to climb out.

But my mother didn't hear me; I saw her figure disappear into the dark house.

In the dining room, Helena placed a jug of water on the table. She was wearing her green apron and a matching hat that kept her hair back. The table looked impressive.

Ann sat opposite me and placed a napkin on her lap.

"Try the mince pies," I said, "they're delicious."

Ann said everything looked delicious. We ate the sandwiches, and popcorn; we ate cheese straws and corn curls and salty, oily peanuts. There were little guava tarts with powdery sugar on the top and marshmallow squares in pastel shades. We were too full to eat the cake, so I said we could wait a while and eat it later. The lime-juice was sweet and cold, and we drank so much it made us bloated. Ann said it was the best lime-juice she had ever tasted.

"You must tell my grandmother that," I said, "she'll be pleased."

I knew my grandmother was still in the kitchen. When I

called her and she didn't come, I excused myself from the table.

My mother and grandmother were standing by the screen door.

"Ann likes your lime-juice," I said. "Are you going to come and say hello?"

My grandmother looked troubled; her pale face was worried and suddenly older. I thought something had happened.

"Is everything all right?"

My mother looked at me in a strange way. Then she looked away at the clock above the stove.

"Your grandfather will be back soon," she said. "Go and look after your guest."

In my room, I showed Ann my favourite clothes: the striped top and matching skirt I wore when I travelled on the plane, and a glittery strapless top my mother said was much too old for me. Ann ran her hand over the tiny sequins. Pulling down the top of her dress, she held it up to her chest. In the mirror she turned to one side and back to the front again. I thought how sparkly and fancy it looked against her skin.

We sat on the floor and looked through some English magazines. I told Ann I might be a model one day and make lots of money.

On the old tape recorder, I played her my favourite disco tune and showed her the special dance moves my friend had taught me. Ann thought they were funny, but she tried to do them too, and soon we were both jumping up and down and wriggling our hips and swinging our arms as though we were waving flags. Ann showed me a three-step which she said was a typical Trinidad dance.

From the window, I saw my grandfather parking his car in the driveway. He looked up and I waved in the same dancing way, and Ann looked down and waved at him too.

Tired, we lay on the bed. A wind blew the curtains and made them swell like sails.

"I will write, you know," I said.

Ann said she knew I would, and she would write too. Then she looked at her watch and said her father would soon be here.

"Let's go eat the chocolate cake," I said and jumped up from the bed.

I heard his voice from the landing. I could hear the voices of my grandmother and my mother too, but mostly it was his voice, rising above theirs in a way I knew meant he was angry. I made a face at Ann and ran quickly down the stairs. Then I closed the kitchen door so she wouldn't be able to hear.

"Go and wait in the verandah," I said. "I'll bring the cake outside."

I don't know if she heard him say "pickney", and "I want the pickney out of my house." But I'm sure she didn't hear him say he would never bring his granddaughter back to the islands again if all she could find to play with was some pickney from the pool, because by then she was outside. I could see her sitting in the hammock.

"I'll send her somewhere else for holidays; somewhere she can be with children like her."

Ann hadn't finished her cake when her father pulled up in the driveway. She said she must say thank you to my mother, but I told her it didn't matter; they were all busy inside talking about a family problem and I would tell them myself on her behalf.

I kissed her on both cheeks like they do in Europe. Then I said goodbye, and that, if I could, I would try to see her at the pool before I left.

When I turned to go back to the house, Helena was standing by the door. I knew she was going for a walk because she was wearing her afternoon dress. She didn't look upset, but there was something in her eyes that made me feel ashamed.

Upstairs, I folded my clothes and put away the old tape recorder. Then I straightened up the magazines and closed the curtains. On my pillow I could smell Ann's flowery scent.

ALAN

When Luke started to choke, I thought that was the end of him, the end of my life as I knew it, and also, perhaps, my father's life. We were sitting at the dining table with the glass top in the front room; in the middle of the table was a large candle that my mother had forgotten at the back of a cupboard. For some reason my mother never liked to use things up. You could look in her cupboard and, chances are, find exactly whatever you wanted like new and still in cellophane.

"Red is a lucky colour," I'd said, "let's put it on the table."

There were Christmas cards strung above the windows, a plastic, flashing Santa on the wall and, in the far corner of the room, a real Christmas tree that my mother and I had bought in the village. I remember how we stood around in the cold, waiting, until a young boy unloaded a new batch and lined them up at the front of the shop. She pointed to the tallest tree which, when untied, sprung into a broad and shaggy shape. "Just think," she said, as we were driving through the fields towards the house, "if we didn't have this big car, we couldn't carry it home."

Alan had found some old decorations in the garage. My mother said we could keep the tinsel, but there was no point in using old baubles – you could buy such pretty ones now. "We're starting over," she said, when Alan went inside. "May as well do it properly." So we got in the car and drove to Schofields' department store where, while my mother looked for lights, I found baubles and a sparkly angel for the top. She bought crackers to put on the branches and cotton wool to wrap around the base. When Alan saw the decorated tree, he clapped his hands. Then he stood away from it and ran his fingers through his grey hair. "That's the best Christmas tree I've seen in years."

"Do you know how lucky we are?" my mother said, looking around my newly decorated bedroom at the floral curtains and lilac walls. We were standing at the full-length window, which opened onto a small balcony. From there, we could see the bare apple tree and the huge pine tree at the end of the sloping lawn. Later, I thought, I might collect some cones and spray them silver and gold. A light snow was falling and landing on the grass like flour.

"Who'd have guessed?" she said, smiling and shaking her head. I thought how pretty she looked, her deep brown hair tied up, in her jeans and casual shirts, more like an older sister than my mother.

Luke's room was smaller, and the view was different. You could see the square patch of grass and a thin path that led to the gate. It made a creaking sound, especially when someone left it open and the wind blew. Luke had a desk and shelves where he could keep his books; there were coloured beanbags on the floor. That same day, I sat on one and showed him the striped tie I'd bought for Alan, and lavender oil I'd bought for our mother.

"Is that it?" Luke asked.

I said, "Get something else, then," and threw the change onto his bed. He counted the coins.

"There's enough here for some rope."

"Rope?" I said.

"So she can hang herself. Either that, or a red bulb to put in the light."

I don't think my brother knew what he was talking about. Sure, he had heard about prostitutes, but he didn't really know what they did or how they made a living, any more than I knew. I told him: whatever he said came straight out of our father's mouth.

Once a month, my mother put Luke and I on a train to Leeds. We passed through mining villages and big open stretches of land where there were little farms and cottages, and tiny roads like veins. Everything seemed to be brown or green or somewhere in-between. As we approached the centre, we saw grey ugly cubes that were part of an industrial estate, rows and rows of dark terraced houses, and flats in high tower blocks. Sometimes I'd look up at them and think, thank God we don't live there. When the train pulled into the Victorian station, our father was waiting on the platform – usually leaning up against a post or sitting on a bench checking something in the paper.

It was awkward at first. After we said hello, the three of us often walked along the station road in silence like strangers. But then he would take us to the Royal Oak pub over the road from where he lived, and in no time he was chatting to people, and having us meet his friends. My brother played songs on the jukebox, and pushed coins in the fruit machine, and when they ran out our father gave him more. Now and again the fruits made a winning line and Luke cheered. Then our father shouted, "Drinks on you, Luke!" I thought his Irish accent was strong and I wondered if anyone else thought so too. We ate fish and chips and if we were lucky, as a special treat, he bought us an ice cream from a Mr. Whippy's ice cream van parked up on the corner of the street. Sometimes we got a Chinese take-away and went to his house.

On the way back to the station, he would talk in a loud and sentimental way. "Tell your mother, once she's stopped fooling around, to give me a call." I'd want to say, *How can she give you a call when you don't have a telephone?* Or he might say, "One of these days, I'm going to come and get you. Tell your mother to be ready with her bags."

If our mother had known how we spent the day, she would never have let us go. What's the point in telling her, Luke said. She would only get upset, especially if she knew some of the things he said about her. Like that time we were at his house, and I was trying to figure out a way that I could move things around to make more space, and I heard him talking to Luke in the kitchen. "She sold her soul for a posh house," he said. "How's that?" my brother asked, his voice flat and awkward. "In some ways, your mother's a whore, Luke. A lovely whore, but a whore nonetheless." I pulled back the bamboo beaded curtain that separated the two rooms and Luke looked up, and then he looked at our father who didn't seem to notice I was there and carried on dishing out the Chinese rice. Then he gave Luke a fork, patted his blond head and went into the living room.

In the street where my father lived there were washing lines strung between the houses. I had never seen houses like these before. Red brick, back-to-back, with three rooms and a toilet. When I asked him where he bathed, he told me he used the public baths in the city centre because it didn't cost anything and you could go anytime. He said he washed and brushed his teeth in the old kitchen sink. I must have pulled a face because he said, "Don't start getting all high and mighty on me." The streets around there had similar names. Queen Street became Queen Avenue, or Queen Place, Queen Road, Queen Drive, Queen Terrace, and so on. I could never remember exactly where he lived. When Alan took us away to southern Spain for a vacation, I wrote my father a postcard, but didn't know where to send it, so I took a chance and put "road." And by some small miracle it turned out to be right.

My mother came back from the Spanish resort with a dark tan and an assortment of leather goods. I had never seen her so happy. It wasn't the kind of happiness she had when she was in Trinidad, the kind that comes from a sense of belonging and sure footedness. It was quite different, and it made her seem alive and hopeful. For the first time in years, apart from Luke, she didn't have to worry about a thing.

When Luke came home from school, he stayed in his room or watched television in the den. During mealtimes, he hardly spoke, unless (and this was very obvious) our mother mentioned someone he used to know or a place we used to visit. And then he talked in a free and open way. But if she asked him a question about anything to do with our present life – his new school or a friend in the village where we now lived – he gave clipped one-word answers. Now and again, I saw Alan looking across the table at my brother as though he wanted to say something harsh. I told Luke: whatever you try to do to break them up will only bring them closer together. This, of course, was not true. There were times, rare times, when Alan raised his voice at my mother, and it was usually because of something Luke had or hadn't done.

Luke shouted in his sleep. I couldn't understand what he said, but when I went into his room, he was often thrashing about, as if he was having a fit or a fight with someone. Every now and then he talked about running away.

"How far do you think you'll get before the police find you? You might make it into town, and then what?"

"I could stay with Dad," he'd say.

"The authorities will only bring you back." He knew that was true; social services would not have allowed him to live in our father's house.

"I can always ask Grandpa to send me a ticket and I'll go and live in Trinidad."

"You're twelve years old," I said. "When you grow up you can live where you like."

Sometimes I looked at Luke and I remembered a small child, in Sligo, playing on a beach with his father. And my mother and I searching for razor shells on the other side

– climbing over worn, copper-coloured rocks with pools
where the water was trapped. Mostly, I remembered blue
empty skies – you could always tell when rain was coming,
gather up cups, plates, the big green tartan blanket, and
make it back to the car before it fell. If the sea was smooth,
my father picked up Luke, put him on his shoulders, and
waded into the cold, silvery water. It was nothing like the
warm, turquoise sea in Trinidad, but, my father said, it
was good for him. Toughened him up. If the waves were
rough, we sat together on the sandy bank and watched them
exploding onto the silky shore, their white spray blowing
up high over the rocks. Sometimes, my mother brought her
8mm camera and she made a short movie we could watch at
home on a projector.

When my mother first mentioned his name, and I asked
who Alan was, she said: "Alan is a place where you can put
your head." Even though I didn't quite understand what
she meant, I knew she'd been unhappy for a while. Apart
from the cold weather – my mother was always complaining
about the cold, which made her ache for Trinidad – by then
my father was rarely at home. Late at night I'd hear the front
door open, then heavy and deliberate steps as he slowly
made his way up the narrow stairs. Then he'd stumble on
the dark landing, come into our bedroom and turn on the
light. He'd stand there for a long time – as though trying to
figure out who the sleeping children were.
      Once Luke saw him swaying over the bed like a ghoul. He
said, "What are you doing, Dad?" frightened that his father
might fall on top of him. Dad mumbled something about
the bathroom, staggered to the dresser, opened a drawer and
peed over Luke's sweaters. Finally, he would try the door to
the room he shared with my mother, which at that hour was
often bolted. Sometimes he shouted or kicked against it. In
the morning, we would find him on the sofa sprawled like

someone washed up on the beach – a smell of stale liquor pouring out of his open mouth.

He hadn't always been this way. There was a time when my father held a manager's position in a local textile company. In those days, he left the house early in the morning and was always home in time for dinner. On weekends, when the days were bright, my mother packed a picnic and drove the four of us out to Strand Hill, or we walked in the quiet lumpy hills above the town. Now and again my father played drums with a local jazz band and sometimes my mother took us along to watch, though I can't remember much about this. Everything, my mother said, was as it should be, and if her family hadn't lived on the other side of the Atlantic Ocean but right there in Sligo town, she would have been fine. But my father was one of many workers who were made redundant. My mother didn't know this until weeks later, when she received a telephone call from someone at the factory wanting to speak to her husband.

"Where do you go?" she asked, when he came home that evening. "Where do you go every day?" My father didn't answer; he took off his coat, lay on the sofa and closed his eyes.

Once my mother knew this, everything changed. With nothing to hide my father behaved as he liked: he slept all morning, then went out around noon, and came back late at night. He didn't seem to want to talk about their problems or look at the future. My mother said he'd rather spend all day drinking in O'Callaghan's. She didn't know what to do. She talked about returning to Trinidad, but Trinidad was in a high state of emergency and the Black Power revolution had just begun. On the telephone, my grandfather said people were leaving in droves, terrified. He listed families my mother knew about, families that had packed up their houses and fled to Miami. It wasn't safe for white people, he warned. Now was not the time to come home.

"Don't worry," I said, sitting on the edge of my mother's bed, feeling like fish were swimming in my stomach. "Something will happen."

That winter night, when my father rang, he didn't want to speak to Luke or me like he usually did; he wanted to talk to our mother. He told her that he wanted to kill himself; that without us his life was no longer worth living and what was the point. He might tie himself to the train tracks, or hang himself, or swim out to sea or shoot himself in the mouth. Then, he said, *It's Christmas. I have nowhere to go.* Now and again, I heard my mother say something like, *Things will work out, or don't worry.* She said his name a lot, and she also said please, please. When she put down the phone she started to cry and rushed from the room. Alan brought her back and sat her down.

Alan said that it was wrong for anyone to be alone at this time of year, and if my father really did not have anywhere to go, then it was obvious he should come here and spend Christmas with his children. My mother was twirling strands of dark hair around her finger, and she was looking around the room as though she was trying to imagine my father in it. "This is our first Christmas together," she said, "I want it to work out."

That Christmas morning we each took turns to open our gifts. Alan gave Luke an aeroplane with a remote-control box that could fly as high as the house, and for a moment, I thought he looked genuinely pleased. He said, *Thank you*, in a way that I had never heard him speak to Alan before. Alan said he would wear the tie as soon as he was back at work. "That's a serious tie," he said, and smiled, his big hands folding it into a scroll. He gave my mother many things: a hairdryer, a make-up kit, underwear.

"You can hide them in your wardrobe," Luke joked, and

my mother looked happy. I thought, who knows, today everything might just be okay.

The turkey was cooked by the time my father arrived. Luke must have seen him coming through the gate because, quick as a sparrow, he flew downstairs and before I could reach, opened the door. He brought him into the warm living room, where, for the second time, my father met Alan. They shook hands and Alan said, "Glad you could come." Then my mother came in wearing her new pink mohair dress, and my father looked at her as though she was a celebrity. And it's true, she did look glamorous that day. Her long hair was flicked on one side like one of Charlie's Angels, and she was wearing a strong mauve lipstick. My father said, "Thanks" and she gave him a wide smile and I was glad. Then he put his hand on the back of my head and said to Alan, "Before you know it, the months go by, and they've shot up."

I was going to show him around the house. I wanted to show him my bedroom and the view from there of the sloping garden, but Alan said there was time for that later. Then my father went over to the tree, and I noticed his same grey corduroy trousers, and navy sweater with patched sleeves and I thought, *It's Christmas, you could have worn something else.* He was wearing a knitted hat, and I wished he would take it off. Still, I thought, with all that my father is pretty good looking and if I could get my mother to trim his beard it would make such a difference.

"Like something out of a magazine," he said, looking at the tree and he signalled to my mother.

"Yes," she said, "we all did a little bit."

"Apart from Luke," I said. Luke didn't say anything; he was sitting on the sofa, watching.

Alan offered my father a drink.

My father nodded and said, "It's bitter out there. The wind." He went to the window and looked out. The snow was coming down sideways in fat flakes. "Sit by the radiator," my mother called through the hatch. Alan held up a bottle of whiskey and when my father nodded, poured some into a glass with ice. I thought, that's a big mistake. But my father drank slowly and asked reasonable questions about Alan's business – his plans for the new showroom, staff management, Christmas sales. And Alan talked to my father easily, as though they were old friends. I was amazed.

When my mother called Alan to carve the turkey, and he went into the kitchen, my father had already finished his drink. Without saying anything to Luke or me, he went to the cabinet and filled up his glass. He quickly drank the whiskey. Then he filled his glass again. Then again. My brother looked uneasy.

"Dad," I said. Then, "Please don't." My father shook his head as if I was being ridiculous.

We had just started eating when Alan opened a bottle of wine. He poured my father a glass and I gave my mother a look. She glanced at Luke who was sitting opposite her and Alan, looking down at his plate. No one was speaking and no one looked particularly happy. I thought about playing some carols on the sound system, but I wasn't sure if it was the right thing to do.

It started like this: Luke cleared his throat, and then coughed. He took a mouthful of water, and then he coughed again. My mother stopped eating and said, "You okay?" Luke nodded, and he coughed some more. Then my father hit Luke on the back, and he coughed harder. I thought Christ Luke, stop fooling around or someone here is going to freak out. He pointed at his throat, and I could see he was trying hard to swallow. My father hit him again, but this time, Luke pushed away from the table, and kicked back his legs so the chair went from under him. Next thing, he was kneeling on the carpet, coughing and coughing and coughing.

Our mother jumped up from the table and said, "Luke. Jesus."

Alan said, "Get him up. We need to get him up." And he went to where my brother was now curling over and stooped down to pull him up.

"Leave him alone," my father said. Then in a booming voice, "Leave my son alone." Alan looked up at him as if he could not quite believe what he was hearing.

"Please don't start," my mother cried. She looked as though she was going to burst. "Not now, not now, please." Luke spat something onto the floor; it looked like a piece of potato. There was some liquid too, which I thought must have been mostly water. But he was still coughing, and now his face was round and big like a giant blueberry.

"Move out of the way," Alan said, standing now and glaring at my father. Before I knew what was happening, my father had pushed him and Alan stumbled back against the table, knocking over some glasses and the candle which I blew out at once. I thought, *God, don't let Luke die, don't let him die*. Then Alan was up again, and my father was right there – his fist back and square. I thought this is it and I don't know why but I said, "Police!" When the blow came down Alan ducked like someone in one of those old black and white films, and this time it was my father who fell crashing into the table sending things flying off the ends and onto the floor, cracking the glass table right through like a fork of lightning cracking through the sky. My mother shouted "Christ" and pushed her fingers up in her hair.

Alan pulled Luke from the floor. His head was loose, and his blue eyes rolled back like marbles. He was gasping now like someone drowning. Alan quickly turned him around and gripped him under his rib cage. Then, locking his big hands together, he made his arms into a vice, and in one sudden, upward movement, squeezed my brother hard. Luke jerked forward, spluttered, and the meat shot out of his mouth. When Alan held it up, I couldn't believe how small it was.

By now Luke was sitting upright, and his face was red and streaked with tears. He was shivering too, like this had all taken place outside in the snow. While my mother held him, I put my head against his back as though it was a rock. I could hear his heart like hooves on a track. Outside, the gate creaked as it blew in the wind, and I knew my father had gone.

SANDRA

Helena used to say that if you want to give your soul a fright, fly over Haiti and look down. The dried-up landscape comes at you like a thousand ghosts. She said, too, that Trinidad had a dark cloud floating above it, which is why we had so much trouble. I didn't know about that. Trinidad was where the sun made you brown and happy, where my mother's family lived and where my mother should live, and one day probably would. I was thinking about these things when our plane landed at Piarco.

This was not a holiday. Just two days before, we'd heard that my grandfather had a heart attack in the car park of Gulf City shopping plaza in San Fernando. My grandmother had phoned, "I can't cope on my own. You must come." So, my mother, right there and then, telephoned a travel agency in Leeds and booked two tickets. I would have to miss school, she said. It was understood that Luke would stay with Alan. We weren't sure how long we would be gone.

On the aircraft steps, the heat rushed at my face, so much so that I turned around and looked at my mother and she said, "Jeeze Louise, feel that." It was like nothing in England. Even the hottest day in a scorching summer, when tarmac melted and grass turned brown and dry like hair, didn't come close to this heat.

Sandra, my mother's cousin, had arranged to meet us. She was waiting in a small crowd at the arrival point. When she saw us, she raised her hand, waved and pushed through the people in front of her. She looked different. Her hair was shorter, and her face thinner; she didn't look like a girl anymore. She looked like a woman, of twenty, at least. Sandra put her arms around my mother and then around me, and I was glad she was there. Then she took my mother's suitcase, and my mother took mine and we made our way to my grandfather's Ford estate car. She said my grandmother was making dinner, and she told us, as we probably knew, she had been hanging out at the house, helping with this and that, because she'd had her own problems recently, and my grandmother was a very healing person.

As we drove along the highway, I looked at the pointed hills, dark and then light. I thought that no matter how many times I went away and came back, the hills would be there. I thought about the houses on stilts in the fields that looked as if they might fall down. In the rainy season the fields looked like lakes and the stilts didn't seem as high. I thought about Luke and wondered what he was doing at that minute.

Sandra turned off the cooler and opened the window. Over on the bank at the roadside, a group of vultures circled above a bloated dog. It was a small, young dog. There were often dead dogs on the road, swollen and smelly. Once they got onto the highway, it was difficult for them to find their way back. The dog was lying with its legs in the air, stiff, like it was made of plastic.

Sandra said, "This place. Only in Trinidad."

Ahead, cars were slowing down and backing up. Someone shouted, "What's going on?"

Sandra said, "It looks like there's been an accident." Something was definitely holding us up. My mother said, "This is all we need." Soon, people were stopping and getting out of their cars; some of them were walking up the lanes of the highway. When a man passed by from ahead of us, Sandra leaned out of the window and asked, "What's happening?" He didn't know exactly, but yes, apparently there had been an accident near Kentucky Fried Chicken Drive In.

"Someone real screaming up there," he said.

Sandra shook her head and turned off the engine. "I've had enough of screaming."

"What do you mean?" asked my mother.

And then, as the sky grew dark, and the hills disappeared into their darkness, and people got out of their cars, and walked along the highway to see what was happening, and went back to their cars and waited, Sandra told my mother the story of Shipper. I closed my eyes but listened hard, especially when Sandra lowered her voice.

Six months ago, when she was feeling unhappy, Sandra had read about a meditation course held in a school in Vistabella. A man called Shipper, a spiritual teacher, and his English wife ran the classes. The newspaper advertisement promised "Peace of mind, awareness, spiritual abundance and fulfilment."

The "beginners" classroom was no bigger than my grandparents' veranda; wooden chairs in a half circle, with a separate chair at the front; desks were piled up in a corner. There was a ceiling fan in the room, but it didn't work. There were only two men, and they didn't look very comfortable. A blonde woman was sitting on the far side with her hands open, as though waiting for someone to put something in them.

Sandra had imagined Shipper's wife would look like my mother, or like my mother's English friends, but when the woman walked in, she looked like no one she had ever seen. The woman wore a full-length flowery dress with a high collar, long sleeves, and a frilly hem. Her fair hair was pinned at the back, and free strands fell about her face. Her skin was pale and freckled, as though it had never seen the sun.

"Like sand on snow," Sandra said. "Get a bit of sand throw it in the snow and there she was."

The woman, Frances, went around the group, looking at each person for a long time. She kept her arms by her side and her eyes, cold and grey, shifted from one person to the next. When she came to Sandra, Frances quickly looked away. Sandra followed her gaze and saw she was looking at a picture of Jesus on a wall. It was crooked. When she looked back, the woman was still staring at the picture. At last, Frances sat down and closed her eyes.

Sandra went to these classes once a week, and there were the same people, apart from one or two who didn't come back. Now, when Frances came in, they all sat down and looked at her in the same way that she looked at them. After a while, although they still seemed cold, Sandra didn't mind looking in Frances' eyes; it was part of being detached. Mostly they meditated for twenty minutes, and then they talked about what happened. Some people saw light or felt themselves drifting into other realms of consciousness. Others started to cry when they talked about someone who had died, or they saw themselves as a child, and Frances would say, "Put your arms around your inner child."

One blonde woman would be rocking back and forth. "What happened to her? my mother asked. "Why was she rocking?"

"She had some troubles," Sandra said. "Like everyone who showed up there."

Sandra knew she wasn't meditating right, because she never felt peaceful. When you meditate, you're meant to close your eyes and empty your mind. But when she tried to do this, it was impossible. She'd remember a movie she wanted to see, or someone's telephone number went round and round. She tried to let her thoughts go like Frances said: *Let them go like leaves in the wind*. But then she started thinking about leaves, and where they might blow, and she'd find herself in a dark wood, so she'd have to get back to the room as quickly as she could, and look at the wall, at the crooked picture of Jesus.

Whatever happened, she always ended up in the same place. Once, when Frances asked her what she had seen during the meditation, she didn't know what to say, so she said she saw Jesus. Everyone thought that was very special.

Sandra didn't meet Shipper until the end-of-term party at the house where he and Frances lived. Shipper was supposed to be more spiritually advanced than Frances. He could see auras and angels. He could tell if you'd been a princess, or a gypsy, or an African slave in a previous life.

"They had parties?" my mother said. "What kind of parties? In their home?"

Sandra described how the house was white and small, with a sloping silver roof, and burglar proofing over the windows. A mango tree made the front yard dark, and though the grass was short, the bushes with blue flowers were high and wild.

When she arrived, Frances was in the kitchen, stirring a large silver pot. She looked hot and tired. But she smiled in a cheerful way, said hello and told Sandra to go into the yard where Shipper was lighting a fire. There were drinks out there in a cooler. She apologised for the mess; they hadn't had chance to unpack.

Apart from the boxes stacked along the passageway, and the boxes and furniture covered with white sheets in the garage, the house was almost bare. In the living room there was a sofa and an American recliner chair. The tiles on the floor were grey and peeling, and the thin curtains were also grey. Outside, the blonde woman was laughing, and Sandra realized she had never heard her laugh before.

Someone from the group came up behind her and said, "Come on, dreamy girl."

I knew Sandra didn't like being called dreamy, but it was something people often said about her. Dreamy, romantic, naive, hippy dippy.

Shipper was shorter than she had imagined, and his dark

hair was almost long enough to make a ponytail. He came across the grass towards her. He was wearing blue, rolled-up trousers and a yellow T-shirt. His feet were bare.

"You must be Sandra," he said, taking her hand. "I hear you saw Jesus in a meditation."

Sandra said his eyes were lively. "He reminded me of a movie star, but I couldn't remember who."

Most of the afternoon was spent sitting in the shade. Some people were talking in the kitchen, others in the veranda where a table was laid with plates and salads and fruit. When Frances wasn't serving drinks or carrying dishes to and from the table, she was hovering around the guests, making sure they were all right. Her long white dress made her look like an apparition. She complained about the heat, and cooled herself with a heart-shaped straw fan.

Sandra chatted with the blonde woman, who was called Angela. She had lived in England and Sandra asked her if she'd ever been to Yorkshire. She told Angela about us and how we came back to Trinidad almost every year for the summer holidays. Angela talked about English department stores which, she said, were sort of like malls, and how she missed being able to go in and find what you want in ten minutes, not like in Trinidad where you have to drive all over the island to find a pair of shoes.

Sandra remembered a young, dark-skinned woman who was holding a watermelon coming to the party, and thinking, *What a lot of women in one little house.*

They had a meditation session, and she was surprised to find Shipper looking at her. His eyes seemed smaller, and less friendly than before, and for a moment she felt afraid and looked around but everyone else in the group had their eyes closed and were breathing deeply. But then he smiled, and she felt a strange heat rise. "You know, like when you see someone you know and you're glad to see them."

"Yes," my mother said. "I know exactly what you mean."

Shipper's face looked almost holy, like old religious paintings of saints and apostles and Sandra had wondered if he could be an apostle, one that came back to put things right.

My mother said, "Oh Sandra!"

Looking back, Sandra said she wondered if Frances would ever have told her about the job if she hadn't seen Shipper in the grocery store. She was standing at the check-out when he appeared. She said she was sure she blushed, because at that moment, she was about to bite into a Tunnocks caramel bar that she hadn't yet paid for, and she was wearing a striped boob tube that had slipped down low.

Shipper asked if his wife had spoken to her about the job, and told her that Frances had all the details. Give her a call. Then he pointed at her hand where the Tunnocks bar had melted, and the chocolate was seeping through her fingers. Sandra said her face went hot like she'd eaten a chilli pepper.

It turned out that Frances hadn't told Sandra about the job because there hadn't been a spare minute. Also, she didn't think Sandra would be interested; it was dirty work. There were boxes to unpack, rooms to clean, and walls to paint. In the afternoons, Sandra would work in the small office; follow up any interest from potential investors with phone calls or typed letters. Frances said Saturdays were never a good time to call people at home, because they had things to do. She had tried telling Shipper this, but he wouldn't listen. The idea was to publicise the meditation programme. She would do the job herself, at least the sales part, only weekends were impossible. Of course, Sandra would have to find a way to get there, too.

"She obviously didn't want you doing the job," my mother said.

"Exactly right."

I checked my watch and saw that we hadn't moved for more than half an hour. It was dark outside, and I had no idea where we were. I was tired, keen to be in my grandmother's house – and I was hungry. Still, Sandra was keeping us entertained.

Sandra lit a cigarette, took a long pull and exhaled through the car window. Then she told us about the job, and how Frances would be at the store and Shipper working with a client when she started on unpacking the books. They were books with unusual titles, like *Metaphysics in the New Age*, and *Jesus in the New World*, and *Mind, Magic and Mysteries*. There were diagrams with rainbow colours used to illustrate different bands of energy, and how they flow around the body, and photographs of men floating in the air and a child with long hair who bled from her wrists. Exercises told you how to locate your higher power, how to find your destiny. A drawing of a palm had each line marked and labelled. She couldn't find her head line and her destiny line was broken into dashes. But according to the diagram, she was going to have two male children, and hardship in her middle years.

When Frances came home, she'd call Sandra to help in the kitchen and there she talked about how she came from a middle-class family in Wales and had met Shipper on a retreat, just after she finished university. She'd known he was special the moment she met him; there was something both ancient and modern about him. A mystical teacher had told Shipper he was there to do important work, and he decided to forget about his law degree and start training in metaphysical practices. They were married in a field of blue flowers. After the ceremony, someone sang "Stairway to Heaven", and they jumped over a stick like pagan people. If they ever were to separate, the stick would be broken in two. It was that simple. The stick was in the bedroom. Sandra said she hadn't expected it to be so long.

Every week, while Frances was at the store and Shipper was working, Sandra unpacked boxes. When Frances came home, she would tell her what to put where. Sometimes

Shipper came into the room and if Frances wasn't there, he'd sit on the American recliner chair and ask Sandra questions: about her dreams, her beliefs, what she wanted to be. After a while, he'd get up and go back to work.

Eventually, the books were on the shelves, the record player was working, all the albums were stacked, cushions and pillows unwrapped, ornaments and vases dusted and wiped, pots and pans and special cutlery put away, photograph albums placed in drawers, sheets and towels in the laundry cupboard, pictures were on the walls and tools were out in the shed. Frances helped her stack the empty boxes by the gate. When Shipper saw them, he called Sandra a star and she said no one had ever called her that before.

Sandra told the couple she thought the walls in the living room should be painted yellow, so when the sun came in it would be lovely and gold. Frances said it must be pale, like a daffodil yellow, nothing too heavy but Shipper said, *Let Sandra decide*, and he'd tousled her hair and said, *Don't you think so, Frances?* Frances didn't say anything, but when she drove out to go to the store, the car made a screeching sound. Shipper said that the gears were giving trouble. Then he sat her down on the recliner chair and told her about the snake sleeping at the bottom of her spine.

Shipper said everyone had a snake there. The snake needed to wake up, because, when it was awake, everything would change. It would uncoil and rise through her body, making its journey through different energy centres. The journey might take months or years, but each stage was marked by distinct changes in consciousness associated with particular psychic powers. Her energy was blocked, but he could help her release it. Then he looked at a place below her stomach and put his hand there. "He told me to breathe. Breathe. So, I did," Sandra said.

Sometimes, when Frances was out at the store, Shipper would come into the kitchen where she was washing or cleaning or putting away dishes. He led her to the recliner chair, where she lay down and closed her eyes. Then he played music with chimes and bells, and spoke in a calm, slow way.

"He told me to imagine the snake waking up, uncoiling, rising through my spine, pushing through the centres and bursting out the top of her head."

Now Sandra started to speak very softly. I kept my eyes closed and kept still so they would think I was asleep.

Sometimes, to wake the snake up, she opened her legs, and he put his hand inside. At first it felt strange but after a while there didn't seem to be anything unnatural about this. She let him blow healing white light into the place where the snake slept. She took off her vest, and he put one hand on her bare back and the other on her heart. Breathe in the white light, he'd say. Breathe. Sometimes, she worked the light with her fingers; that way, Shipper could make sure the energy was moving upwards.

Shipper told her that when he was inside her, she became other girls, girls with different eyes and different skin. She was a geisha; an African slave; a maiden from Denmark; an Icelandic princess. There had been lifetimes in Egypt and Japan. He'd say, *Look at you, like a maiden*. Or, *Look at you, like a princess*. Sometimes he became someone else too: a young boy, or a Pharaoh, or a soldier from the war.

Sandra said she had to tell him not to get it on her clothes. Apparently, the first time, it seemed to be everywhere, like thick glue: on her mouth, in her hair, on the front of her dress. I did not understand this, but my mother sounded surprised, even disgusted.

She said, "Where was his wife when this was going on?"

Sandra said Frances was usually in the yard watering the young trees or cutting the grass or the hedge, so they went into the office where there was a lock on the door. They lay on the floor, or perched on the desk, or balanced on a chair. Sandra knew his wife couldn't see what they were doing because the curtains were closed, but when she heard the hose, or the clipping of the shears, she felt uncomfortable. Shipper said she mustn't feel that way or think about all that. Frances had her own karma to work out. At some level she knew what was happening, and at some level she was in agreement with their relationship. Otherwise, how could it happen?

My mother said, "Oh my God."

If Frances knew there was something happening, she never let on. Only once, when she saw Frances behind her in the mirror in the bathroom, while she was combing her tangled hair, she'd called out to her but Frances didn't say anything, but walked away down the corridor like someone in a dream.

Then one afternoon, when Francis was out, she and Shipper were lying uncovered on the large bed. He was telling her about angels, and how, every so often, they incarnate in families in order to heal them. He said they leave signs when they go; they communicate through nature: through a bird singing outside your window, or a sweet scent, a trail of petals, a white feather. He was leaning over, looking at her.

"I was thinking I should take a shower," she told my mother. She knew Frances would soon be home and there were things to do in the kitchen and she still hadn't folded the clothes or washed the floor. From nowhere, a strong wind blew into the room. The curtains swelled and the door slammed.

Shipper sat up and looked around and said there was a spirit there.

She'd asked him what kind of spirit and pulled up the sheet, suddenly feeling cold.

For a moment Shipper was quiet. "He's a tall man with fair hair," he said. His voice was calm and certain. "He's here because of you."

She'd drawn the sheet under her chin.

Shipper told her not to be afraid, and he started to talk

in riddles. She didn't know if Shipper was talking to her or the spirit, because he was looking at a place near the dresser. He told her the spirit was harmless and not there to hurt anyone.

She'd wanted to ask, *Why is he here?* but couldn't speak. Then Shipper got up and stood in the narrow shaft of light coming through a gap in the curtains. He raised his hands as if he was lifting something, and then he closed his eyes. He was speaking in a low voice, and she couldn't quite catch what he was saying, but it sounded like a kind of prayer or chant. She heard the words God and Love, but that was all. He stood like that for what seemed like a long time; his arms above his head, holding something she couldn't see, while she stayed still under the sheet.

She'd started to cry, and Shipper held her in his arms, and she'd cried, and cried, until she couldn't cry anymore.

She told him about her father, and how when she was a baby, he had left Trinidad and gone to Guyana, looking for gold. She couldn't remember too much about him, only that he was tall, and he had blonde hair, and he came back now and then with colourful gifts and stories about jaguars, giant anteaters, butterflies as big as his hands, but mostly he stayed away. For many months he panned for gold near Marshall Falls with another man. One day a telegram arrived informing her mother that pieces of her husband's mauled body had turned up on the banks of the Essequibo River. They never sent his body back. Her mother had always wondered if he wasn't dead at all, but living somewhere in South America.

Shipper told her not to be sad; people only die so they can be reborn; that's the whole point. She had to let her father go, let him go. Then he could be free to follow his karma.

"That's a big deal, Sandra," my mother said. "That's a really big deal."

Then, everything changed when Angela organised a

holiday for the group over on the other island. The boat was
leaving at seven. By the time she'd arrived at the docks, there
were crowds making their way along the platform to the
lower deck. She wasn't sure how she would find the others.
Her bag was heavy with vegetables. She had a pineapple, too,
with its top cut off so it wouldn't catch on her clothes.

The group was gathered on the top deck. Frances was
sitting on a bench surrounded by bags and boxes. Angela
was leaning against the rail and watching the passengers
below. She was wearing a bright orange dress and her hair
looked like it had been set in curlers. Sandra told everybody
hello and put her bag down.

Mina, the blonde woman, was complaining about the
heat. Her turban was brown and gold and it matched her
long dress. There were a couple of women she hadn't
seen before. Then she saw Angela was talking intensely to
Shipper, who was looking up at the clear night sky. The sea
was huge and black, except where the thin moon tossed a
silver glow. There was a strong, salty breeze.

She hadn't noticed the man at first. Not until someone
pointed him out. He was wearing ordinary clothes: trousers
and a shirt and sandals. His hair was greased and slicked back
from his fine-boned face. He didn't seem to be bothering
anyone, but he was looking at Frances in a strange way. In
fact, he was staring at each member of the group, but he
was looking at Frances more than anyone else. She thought
Frances looked very pale, more pale than usual, as if she was
unwell. She looked around for Shipper but couldn't see
him. Mina said he had gone downstairs to buy something
to drink.

"I couldn't understand why he would go off to buy a
drink," Sandra said, "when we had a whole cooler of sodas,
right there. I went down to the lower deck to find the
bathroom and see if he was there."

The lower deck was overcrowded. People were sitting

against the walls of the boat, and some were lying on mats. It was hot. Some were smoking, and some were drinking rum or scotch. Bottles rolled about the floor. Sandra said she'd been worried she might fall over. Near the bathrooms the smell was so bad, she couldn't go inside. A lady said, *Don't bother with that, miss. Find a corner somewhere to pee. It's dark, no one will know.*

Sandra was about to go back upstairs when she saw Angela and Shipper. Shipper's hand was cupping her breast; his mouth was fastened on her neck. She'd called out to them, and they'd looked at her as though she was a lunatic.

On the top deck, she saw Frances was sitting with her back pressed against the side of the boat. She had her head between her knees and was trying to breathe under Mina's instruction. Her forehead was wet, and her hair was sticking about her face. When Shipper came back to the top deck, he helped her up. She looked so weak the wind might throw her down. The staring man had long gone.

When they landed, while Angela and Shipper went to find a taxi, Mina held Frances's arm and supported her back; she tried to fan her pale face with a book.

Then Mina said they'd have to find a priest. Sandra asked why, and Mina told her it happens sometimes that someone comes along, like the man on the boat, and they are full of dark energy. They try and take you over. It's a kind of possession.

Then Frances started to groan, and her head flopped forward like a puppet's, and they propped her up against the nearby wall. A trail of saliva ran down her chin. Sandra said it reminded her of a slug. Then Angela and Shipper came back and said they had to take two cars.

By the time they reached the villa, Frances was shaking and white; her eyes were glassy and she was speaking in a garbled way. Shipper carried her inside and laid her down on the sofa while everyone stood around and watched.

Someone gave him a blanket. Sandra said she didn't know what to do, so she sat by the door and looked out.

"I thought," she said, "if I can think about the flowers on that vine, if I can think about the lady of the night, then everything might be okay."

But Frances started singing a hymn in a high voice, and she was up, and standing with her arms outstretched. Shipper was trying to push her down. He told Frances to breathe in the light. But he sounded unsure, and he looked afraid. Frances began to sing louder, so the tune became distorted. Sandra said if she hadn't picked up some of the words, she would never have known it was "All things bright and beautiful".

Angela tried to console Frances. But Frances looked at her as though she was a demon. Angela ran outside. Then Frances pointed at Mina and her eyes went into dark slits.

"I thought," Sandra said, "Oh God she's going to rush at Mina. But she didn't. Instead, she turned to me and shook her head like a horse shaking off heat or flies. Then Frances fell on her knees and began to cry."

Sandra said she ran out of the room, but even from the end of the road Frances sounded like an animal in pain. She could still hear her crying when she reached the beach.

★

That night, our journey from Piarco to my grandmother's house took three and a half hours. When we passed the white Toyota car, it looked as though it had been hit with a giant hammer. We heard later that two people in the car – a couple on their honeymoon from London – had survived.

ROXY

When I first saw Roxy, she was sitting on the wing of the Avro 748, abandoned on a large piece of land at the back of my grandmother's house. Ten years old, wearing a yellow T shirt, denim shorts, her dark hair blowing in the breeze. Most of the plane's insides had been taken out, but there were still some seats, and the cockpit had switches and levers you could fool around with. Roxy, chief air stewardess, walked up and down the centre aisle with an imaginary trolley, and sometimes came up front to tell the pilots – Ray, her brother, and Luke – where she wanted to go. My mother said it was dangerous in the plane and anything could happen, so I didn't get to play inside, though sometimes without her knowing, I crept through the long grass at the back of the house and crawled in through the emergency exit. Roxy welcomed me aboard with a big smile, checked my boarding pass and directed me to an appropriate seat, or she took me into the cockpit. When she leaned over to buckle me in, I could smell her sea hair and feel her breath on my face. They flew all over the world: America, India, Australia, Africa, Europe…

I hadn't seen Roxy or Ray for some years. But that summer, my mother rented a house on the other island, and they were staying over the road, with their mother. When she saw us pull up in the taxi, Mrs Salazar, thin as a rail, came out and told us to come by when we'd settled ourselves in. My mother told me Mrs Salazar, once a beauty, had married the wrong man. "You can pick and pick and pick until you pick shit."

Mrs Salazar's holiday house had a Japanese style roof, and a veranda with a spectacular view out on the bay. Worth a couple million dollars – my mother had seen it in a real estate window – large paintings on the wall, a thick rug on the vast living room floor, a chandelier. Imported furniture, solid and modern. There were three bedrooms, a long corridor lined with breeze blocks to keep the place cool. There was a TV room – with small windows, a sound system, a vast sofa as soft as a cloud. The sea was right there. Light blue, and then darker blue when you looked faraway. By evening it turned to liquid silver. Boats often came and went and moored in the bay.

Mrs Salazar mixed up a jug of icy lime juice and we sat outside, and she and my mother talked about people they knew. Roxy brought a tray with a dip and potato chips and handed them around. She looked different. At seventeen, she had fine bone structure, geometric cheekbones, dirty green eyes, a small nose, an almost perfect mouth. She had a dimple in her chin which I had forgotten about. A sign of chutzpah, my mother said. I figured this was true; Roxy seemed to me to have a lot of chutzpah. To her mother's dismay, she'd jacked in school and applied for a job as a flight attendant with BWI. I said, "Well, you've certainly had enough experience."

Every morning, we piled into a pick-up truck, and Ray drove us to the beach. Lined with coconut trees, little cabanas, a long jetty with a straw hut, it looked like something from a magazine. We spread our towels on the hot sand, rubbed oil into our skin and lay down. Roxy tanned quickly, and when she took off her bikini top and flipped onto her stomach, I was surprised by how white the triangles of pale skin were. Like sails of a boat, Luke said. I told him he shouldn't be looking. But it was hard not to look at Roxy. When she walked to the water's edge and put her hands on her waist, I thought how shapely she looked in her striped bikini, curvy like a Coca Cola bottle, as my mother liked to say.

Luke gazed at her as if she was made of light. When he wasn't swimming out to the jetty, he hung around our cabana, cracked jokes. He ran his fingers through his long hair, shorts hung low; a bandanna tied around his forehead like John McEnroe. He'd lay his towel next to Roxy's and listen to music. "Have you heard this track?" he'd say, occasionally, offering his headphones, adjusting the wires around her like a stethoscope. I had never seen him like this before. I wanted to tell him to go away, find something else to do. There was another boy called Pedro, and he seemed to like Roxy, too. Roxy helped herself to Pedro's Du Maurier cigarettes. That summer, she taught me how to inhale, how to press the cigarette smoke down into my lungs and breathe it out in a long plume.

Roxy knew how to swim, and her shoulders made you know it. She wasn't afraid of the current when it was strong. Sometimes the water was rough; there were times when waves were 8ft high, and we couldn't get back to shore without getting tumbled. Go beyond the swell, she'd say, and we'd swim out further, and then make our way back in to ride the wave. She'd stay with me until I wasn't afraid to try again. "There's nothing to be scared of," Roxy would say. "It's just water." There were high rocks, and I followed her up them; watched her strong brown legs; her wet hair trailing down her back shiny as oil. Her smile was broad when she got to the top.

If it was too hot, we left the beach early and made our way home. At Roxy's house, we showered, turned on the air conditioner, then lay on her king-size bed. Back then I was reading abridged illustrated stories by Shakespeare. Roxy found reading difficult. "Read to me," she'd say, lolling back. "Your voice sounds like a voice on the radio." It was a blue room with a ceiling fan, and mahogany cupboards, shutters that never quite shut. There was a dresser with curly legs and a fancy mirror, in which I could see our reflection. I liked how we looked. I read *King Lear*, *Othello*, *Midsummer Night's Dream*, and *Hamlet* to her. But her favourite was *Romeo and Juliet*. She could listen to me all day, she said. When Luke asked what we were doing in there all afternoon, I said, not much. Roxy told me Luke was cute, and if she didn't have Lorcan, she might give it a whirl.

I'd heard Lorcan was a ladies' man. Lorcan was handsome like Harrison Ford. Girls came around him like a rockstar. Or as Ray said later, like flies around shit. Roxy had been going out with Lorcan for more than two years. Six weeks before, Lorcan had left for Houston, Texas where he was studying to be a mechanical engineer. He was likely coming back for Christmas, and maybe she would get herself a flight up there some time. She wore a silver necklace he'd given her with a pendant in the shape of a letter L. She put the letter in her mouth, tapped it against her teeth; ran the chain between her lips. After he'd called, Roxy was cheery and bright. I had the feeling she thought Lorcan might save her from something. I didn't know what that something was.

Lorcan called one day when we arrived back from the beach. Roxy said, "Talk to my friend. She's dying to meet you. Say hello!"

Lorcan's voice was surprisingly deep. He had an American accent and yet he'd only been in Houston for a few weeks. Freshwater Yankee, my mother would say.

"I've heard a lot about you," I said.

"Take care of my baby for me."

I said, "Sure. You bet."

Most men weren't worth thinking about, Roxy said. Her father had another woman in West Moorings, and a child with another woman in San Fernando. Once a cheater, always a cheater. I said all relationships seemed to be perilous. Sitting down by the water's edge, with the houses behind us, I told Roxy about my life in England, and how my mother had also been unhappy. I told her about Alan and my father who felt like an outsider. Roxy wished she had my mother instead of hers. Her mother sometimes seemed normal but often took pills – pills to sleep, pills to lose weight, pills to feel happy, pills to think straight. She drank scotch and smoked at least one pack of cigarettes every day. More than once, Roxy had found her mother on the bathroom floor in a pool of vomit.

"I'd rather die," she said; "in a plane crash. Something you can read about in the papers."

"Yes," I said, "me too."

Days were long and hot, and I wanted them to go on forever. At the beach, we bought burgers and chips, washed down with Coca Cola. If the queue was long, we left Pedro and Luke in line and returned to our cabana. After lunch, we walked along the crunchy sand, where the breeze was strong and warm, and I noticed how many people looked at Roxy. My skin was on fire, and it went from red to red-brown to a golden, deep tan. Roxy said my hair made me look like I came from Sweden.

"Look at you," she said, in the fancy mirror. "Look at us. We're made for more. We're made for fame and fortune." She said it like she meant it.

At sunset, while Luke and Pedro fished with tin cans and wire, we sat and watched the sun slide into the sea like a giant gold coin. The beach was rocky, the sand bed was difficult to walk on. But there were often fish, and if they were lucky, they caught cavali or snook. Roxy slit them, gutted them and washed them under the pipe in lime and water. Once, when Luke stood on a sea urchin, Roxy plucked out the pickers and sent him back into the water. "I'll make a man of him yet," she joked. Luke said there was nothing Roxy couldn't do. He wanted to prove to her that he was worth noticing.

It was while we were watching the sun go down that Roxy told me about her father, and how he had done things he should never have done. What things? I asked. "Things," she said, shaking her head, her mouth set hard. It was a new look, an expression I hadn't seen before. One day, she said, she'd go to the police and report him. But maybe not the police in Trinidad, because in Trinidad they knew who her father was – a high court judge who could send a man down. No, she would wait until she was living in USA, and she could go to the American police.

"Why don't you tell them right now?" I said. "I'll come with you."

"No one will believe me."

"I believe you."

Sitting there was beautiful, and I felt lucky to be sitting with Roxy, and to feel that she was able to say these things. The wind dried our hair, and our burnt skin tingled from the breeze. I had a lightness in my heart, and a hope that things would work out all around. I sensed that for Roxy it was different – she was killing time, waiting for her real life to begin. She was dreaming about Lorcan, travelling overseas, becoming somebody. She wanted to start afresh. Island life sucks, Roxy said, and one day she would get out. If not now, then when Lorcan came back. She could travel back up with him. One day they might have a Texan wedding. Cowboy boots under a white gown. Lorcan in a cowboy hat, a bolo tie, Country and Western music, brisket and steaks in Tex-Mex sauce, Margaritas, fajitas. Roxy had it all figured out.

"As long as he doesn't meet someone else."

"Never," I said. "There's no one prettier than you."

In the evenings, we went over to Roxy's house. Her mother was usually watching TV in a long satin robe, her hair in a turban to keep out the frizz. Roxy mixed her mother a drink, then she fixed herself a rum and coke; Pedro and Luke opened a couple of icy beers, and we got down to the serious business of playing cards. Roxy could deal like a croupier. She split the deck in two, put one half in each hand, with the corners overlapping and the cards weaving together. She did it quickly, as if the cards were hot. Luke said she was a total pro. Making the cards into a bridge, she tipped her hands and let them fly from one hand to the other. We played poker with small amounts of money, not caring if we lost – enough to make it feel risky while fun at the same time. I said I'd rather use match sticks. When Roxy said we could always take off our clothes instead, like in strip poker, Luke and Pedro looked at each other as if they were about to hit the jackpot.

The heat had been building for days; everything was dusty and dry. Plants and shrubs were bent over, and my mother said someone should water them, but no one could find a hose anywhere. So, we took pans of water outside and threw them in the bushes and scattered it over the brown grass. I felt sorry for the goats, and the white cows with gigantic horns whose bones were pushing through their skin. I told Roxy that cows in England looked pretty and plump, they were not emaciated and covered in flies like here. She'd been quiet all day, and I wondered, at first, if I had said something to upset her. I wanted to ask, but there was something about her manner that made me feel I couldn't.

We went to the beach, but didn't stay long. Roxy was sick of the sun, she said. She was sick of the beach, the burger bar. On the way back, she stopped off to buy cigarettes and a bottle of rum. I gave her a look. She didn't say anything. I asked her if she wanted me to come over and read and she said no, not that Shakespeare shit.

I didn't know that Lorcan had called and told Roxy it was over, that he had met someone on campus during Freshers week. She was blonde and came from Pensacola, Florida. Her name was Taylor.

For a couple of days, Roxy stayed away. When I called round, Mrs Salazar said she was in the TV room, and she didn't want to talk to anyone. Mrs Salazar looked tired; her eyes were bleary as if trying to focus.

"Has something happened? Is there something I've done?"

"No," Mrs Salazar said. "Roxanne is a moody girl. People don't realise."

It was unusually hot that evening; the sky felt as if it was about to crack open. Mrs Salazar came over to warn us of a storm. Someone had mentioned it in the gas station. The storm was moving in quickly, she said. Strong winds were travelling north from the coast of Venezuela and would be fully with us that night. Put everything away, she said, sun beds, clothes from the line, beach mats. She had a box of candles and two torches, but that was all. She hoped the electricity would stay on. But you never can tell.

"A hurricane?" I asked.

"Well, yes."

I felt excited and nervous. Mrs Salazar suggested we come over to their house. Some of the houses around here were flimsy as hell – a gust of wind and they could blow away, she said.

We all sat around the veranda. Pedro went home to his grandmother's house in Canaan, just in case. Ray said there was no point in fishing. Then he took off in his pickup truck to see his girlfriend, Desiree. Mrs Salazar told him he was foolish. She would rather he stay here.

The air was thick and still. There was no sound apart from the gentle lap of water from the beach below. I went out to check, and saw the sky was heavy and red, and the sea was flat. Roxy was painting her nails, drinking a rum and coke. Mrs Salazar asked Roxy to mix her a drink. She went to the cabinet and found a new bottle of scotch. She asked my mother if she would like a scotch and soda, and my mother said yes, why not. Roxy poured herself another rum and coke, which she drank quickly. It might have been her second or third. Luke sipped on a cold beer. It was a strange atmosphere – and I couldn't tell whether it was strange because of the storm or because of Roxy's mood. Luke was listening to music, but I could feel his eyes on Roxy.

Then the wind started up, and we went inside. Roxy looked out where the casuarinas were starting to bend. I wondered if she was a bit drunk.

"Ladies and gentlemen, we shall be experiencing some turbulence. Please stay seated and fasten your seatbelts."

I laughed and Luke laughed, too.

Now the wind was whipping around the eaves, whistling high through the shutters. I looked through the gaps and saw boats jostling about as if they were made of paper. We played a couple of hands of poker, but no one could concentrate. I looked outside again – the sky was greyish black. Rain was falling now. The wind was lashing at the yard; I could hear a clatter of branches and pieces of debris on the roof. Then the electricity cut out and we were in darkness.

"Oh boy!" I said.

Mrs Salazar said, "I knew it," got up and made her way to the kitchen to find candles. My mother gave me a torch and I used it to flash around the room; the torch kept flickering.

"There's a torch in my room," Roxy said, getting up.

She turned and looked at Luke. He followed her down the corridor.

In the kitchen my mother and Mrs Salazar were looking for batteries. They lit a few candles and positioned them around the living room. Parts of the room were lit and other parts completely black. The wind was coming into the house through the shutters, making a rattling sound. I helped Mrs Salazar to close them. "This damn wood swells in the humidity."

When I opened her bedroom door, Luke and Roxy were leaning against the bedhead. In the pale flickering light of my torch, I saw Luke had taken off his T-shirt.

"What's going on?"

"Want some?" Roxy held up a bottle of rum.

I could see the red glow of her cigarette.

"Not really."

I could make out Luke's shape, Roxy's outline; her flicky hair.

"I thought there was a torch here, but there isn't," Roxy said. Then she said, "Can you fetch some candles?"

I thought she was talking to Luke, but it was to me.

In the kitchen my mother and Mrs Salazar were fixed at the window, mesh overlaid with burglar proofing. Through its diamond shapes our house looked tiny, exposed. Coconut trees were bending as if their long trunks were rubber; fronds blowing like wild hair.

"Jesus, God," my mother said. "This is no joke." A sheet of galvanise had come loose and hung over our doorway like a guillotine.

"We need another torch," I said. "I can't see anything. Are there batteries?" I felt a sense of urgency. I didn't like that I had left my brother with Roxy. I didn't like what they were doing.

My mother gave me some batteries, and I tried to fit them, but it didn't seem to make any difference. I took some candles, made my way back down the corridor. Tiles were wet and slippery from rain now pouring in.

"Be careful," my mother called.

For some reason, when I entered Roxy's room, I said, "Excuse me." I don't know what I expected to find. But in that moment, her entire room was flooded with a violet-white light, and I saw my brother was lying on top of Roxy. I was too afraid to move; my feet stapled to the floor. I wanted to be in England. I wanted to be anywhere but there. Then another violet-white flash. An image from a black and white film: Roxy and Luke, their bodies stuck together. I called out, "Oh God!" Luke said, "Chill," but he sounded irritated. Roxy told him to shush. Then she said his name, as if to soothe him. Then it came again, the violet-white light. Roxy was sitting up, covering herself with something; I saw her tan lines; her startled eyes.

She giggled and then she said something – her words lost in a boom of thunder.

I wanted to say something, but realised it was nothing to do with me. None of this had anything to do with me. "I'll leave you to it," I said, "I'm sorry."

Next day the yard was strewn with branches, garbage, bottles. I had never seen anything like it. There were reports of boats smashed against rocks, roof tops missing, animals wandering in the road. Luke was quiet, and when Pedro arrived, he gave him a look that I knew Pedro understood. Luke was wearing Roxy's necklace.

Later, he said the letter L made him think it was always meant to be.

MANO

I believe it was a good time for all of us, but perhaps it just seems like that when things are going well for you. I was home from England for the summer, and Sandra and I had got into the habit of taking her old car along the highway into Port of Spain, drive right through, and out towards Carenage where the road turns and twists along the coastline. Sometimes cars hit a bend and flew right off the road; some fell into the sea, black as molasses at night.

If the car park was full, we parked on the road, and from there we walked over to the jetty and caught the late-night party cruise on the *Jolly Roger* boat, a franchise Sandra said had begun in Barbados, where there were plenty of tourists. In Trinidad, the boat only operated during the summer months when the young people came home from school or university. Some of these people looked familiar; I had seen them in bars and nightclubs or up at the beach on the other side of the island.

The *Jolly Roger* was impressive. Twenty dollars and you could drink as much rum as you liked. There was loud music and flashing lights up on the deck where DJ Johnny Heartbeat played. Sometimes I saw Roxy; she was usually on her way to being drunk or merry at the very least; dancing, cup in hand, waving her dark hair about like a horse moves its tail. I'd say, "Hey Roxy, what's happening?" And she'd say, "Hey, what's up." I remember seeing Ann Sanchez there, too, dancing a three-step with a red-skinned man in an old-fashioned way. I said, "Way to go, Annie" and she spun around, startled. Then she smiled, let go of the man and put her arms around me instead. She said something about her father and how much she was going to miss him when she went back to London. Now isn't the time to be thinking about your father, I thought.

One time I saw Ray and Pedro. Pedro kissed me for a long time. I must have been quite drunk because when Ray told me about it later, I couldn't remember, though he insisted it was true and offered to ring up Pedro and ask him about it while I listened on the other phone. I told Ray how sometimes me and Sandra got so drunk, I didn't know how we drove home without something bad happening. There were usually a few guys around, and sometimes you might find yourself kissing someone when the slow tunes were playing. It was on the *Jolly Roger* cruise boat that Sandra met Mano.

Mano lived in Morvant, where his father ran a small air-conditioning repair business. He sometimes helped out with deliveries, but apart from that he didn't do too much. He was skinny, tanned and he had sharp, birdlike features. His eyes were green and that made you wander what his mother must have looked like, because you only had to look at Mano to know that his father was Indian. He said his mother was a Canadian hooker and that she was dead, but I guessed that wasn't true. He had ideas about going away to university in England. I told him he shouldn't even think about England; it was way too cold and grey. "Go to Miami," I said, "where life isn't so different." We were standing on the lower deck of the boat when I said this. Sandra took hold of his arm, looked hard into his eyes and said, "Don't listen to her, she doesn't know what she's talking about. I went to Yorkshire, and it was the most beautiful place I have ever seen."

That night, as usual, Sandra was quite drunk. When Mano said he would drive, even though I feared we might be getting ourselves into trouble, I thought we might be safer with him behind the wheel.

I had never been to the tracking station before, though I learned afterwards that it was somewhere to know about. Mano said we were going to have a little adventure, and, before me or Sandra could say anything, instead of taking the main road towards Port of Spain, he made a left turn and drove Sandra's old car up through a dark and unfamiliar back road.

I wasn't afraid at first, but Sandra said that she had heard there were South American guerrillas living in this part of the island. Then she clapped her hands and laughed so much I knew not to believe her. Mano drove slowly, as if we had all night to get there. When I looked behind there was only blackness and I thought, maybe we'd made a big mistake, and in truth, who is this skinny guy? Although the road was smooth, the bush on either side looked wild and thick. I wondered what lived in there.

Mano parked at the top of a hill. In the headlights, I could make out a huge white shape: a tall, round tower with an enormous, curved structure on the top like some sort of receiver. It looked futuristic. Mano said what lucky girls we were, turned off the lights, got out of the car and disappeared into the darkness.

"Jesus," Sandra said. I wondered if we should take the car and shoot back to where we had come from. But Sandra said no. How often did she get to go out and have some fun? "He's okay," she said, "I've got a feeling."

It was almost impossible to see anything beyond the doorway. When Mano lit the first match I could see curved, high, inner walls and a narrow iron ladder reaching up through the middle of the tower.

"Go easy," he said, taking hold of the sides of the ladder. Sandra was standing right behind him. He put his foot on the high step and hauled himself up.

"I can't do this," I said, pulling on the back of Sandra's blouse.

"It's okay," she said. "We'll go slow."

After seven or eight steps, there was a small platform. Here, Mano leaned back and lit another match. He said, "Be careful. Watch for holes." It was true, the platform was quite rotten, and the rusty metal square had small gaps where it had thinned and disintegrated. Sandra put her feet on the thicker parts and slowly shuffled forwards towards the bottom of the next ladder where Mano held out his hand for her to hold, allowing me space to find my own way in the same manner. It was very quiet, and I could hear her breath and my own shallow breath. I had just placed my foot on the first rung of the second ladder when the match went out.

I said, "No. I can't see. I can't see."

Mano said, "Careful."

The next platform was weaker, but when I stepped around the edges where the metal was strongest, it seemed to be okay. It was easier to see now; light was coming in through a large hole at the top. Light from the moon I figured. When I looked down, I couldn't see anything at all and just at that moment, Sandra said, "Whatever you do, don't look down." I watched Sandra's ankles and her sandals, the rubber soles bending with her large feet as she balanced on the final rungs of the little ladder. I thought, if my mother could see me now.

The dish was much bigger than it had looked from the car. The outer edges seemed like those of a gigantic teacup. I crawled up towards the steeper sides, gripping the lines of wire that formed a kind of mesh on the inside, wondering if I might just tip the whole cup over and fall into the sea, which was right there – the whole north coast of Trinidad stretched out, with its black water and tiny sparkling lights like little flecks of glitter. I looked around for Sandra and saw her lying on her back in the basin of the dish, with her legs bent up towards her. She was staring up at a thin pole that jetted from the centre and reached some twenty feet above us at the top of which Mano was poised.

Sandra shouted, "What the hell!"

I thought, this is madness, but then I thought, so what. And I started singing an old song about being on top of the world. Then Sandra joined in, and Mano waved at us in a royal, exaggerated way, as though he was King of Trinidad.

According to the electric clock it was 12.35am. We were listening to lovers rock and slowly cruising through Woodbrook; Sandra said we should look out for some Chinese food. I said nowhere is going to be open now. I was looking out of the window, thinking about how long the drive would take to Morvant, when I saw the cat on the side of the road – a large black and white shape lying under a streetlight at the edge of the pavement. I told Mano to stop the car, and he pulled up just in front of it. "Hold on," I said, climbing out. Sandra said, "Where you going?"

The road was quiet and there were cars parked along one side of the street. Walking towards it, I smelled urine. The blood around its neck was like a collar, a thick red band. Something was coming from its mouth, saliva or vomit, perhaps. I felt my stomach rise and looked away. It was too thickset to be wild, and its fur was longer than that of a typical stray cat. It must belong to someone. I looked at it again; and then, I don't know why, but I looked at my hands. Sandra shouted, "What you doing?" Mano was smoking a cigarette and looking at me. I said, "Hang on a minute", and put my arm up like a signalling policeman.

The house was partially hidden from the road by a large mango tree and a hedge of sweet lime along the front. From the short driveway, I saw the lights were on. There were no cars in the garage, but there was a bicycle and some roller skates propped against the wall. The front door was closed.

Through the screen window I could see a large dining table, a row of silver trophies on a shelf, a television set. I saw a figure moving near an open doorway. "Hello," I said in a loud voice. Then again, "Hello."

The middle-aged woman was heavy; her hair was black and pulled away from her broad face. She was wearing a red nightdress, and her dark eyes were large. She looked at me in a curious, open way. When I asked if she had a black and white cat, she paused and then said yes, and her expression changed. Then an old man, in his seventies perhaps, came from behind and said, "What is it?"

In a calm voice I said, "I'm sorry, I know it's very late. I don't mean to alarm you."

We walked in silence along the driveway and out onto the road, where the lights of a passing car were so bright I had to shield my eyes. I thought, Christ, not again, in front of these people. The body was as I'd left it.

"Oh God," the woman said, "Oh God. Poor baby." She bent down and, lifting the back legs first, raised the limp body into her thick arms. "Oh God," she said. "Why this have to happen?" The head rolled back and hung downwards. The woman held it in place and said, "No. Oh no."

"Let's go in," the old man said, in a small voice. "Let's go."

The woman laid the body on the grassy bank outside the kitchen window where the neon light was making a bright pool. She put her hand to her mouth and said, "Oh God, Cassandra! Where Cassandra?" I didn't hear the screen door open. I looked up and saw a tall girl with long brown plaits standing in the half-light. I thought how pretty she was. Her slanted eyes were large and dark and sleepy. She said, "Mom?"

"Cassandra," the woman said, "Cassandra," and brought her hands up to her face.

The girl walked slowly to where the cat lay. She ran her fingers along the black and white back. She ran them

over and over. She bent down and looked into the staring
yellow eyes. She stroked the bloody fur around the neck,
and mouth. She wiped away the vomit – I could see now
that it was vomit – with the hem of her long T-shirt. Then
she placed her head on the cat's stomach. Her two plaits fell
into the grass.

On the drive back to Morvant, whenever Mano wasn't
changing gears, he held Sandra's hand, or he rubbed his hand
on the top part of her leg. Nobody was saying anything. I
had told them about the cat and Cassandra and how sad she
was, and they didn't seem too bothered about it. I wondered
what they were thinking, and I also wondered if Sandra
had told Mano that she was married and had a little boy
called Joe, and that she wouldn't be able to see him again;
especially someone like him. When we pulled up outside
his tiny house, I looked out of the window at the brightly lit
porch, while Sandra kissed him for a long time. I could see
someone in the window of the house, an obese man wearing
a vest, standing up and looking at a television. I couldn't
imagine what he was watching at that time of the morning.
Watching snow, I thought. Next thing, Sandra was fishing
around in the glove compartment. She scrawled something
down on a piece of paper. Mano took the piece of paper, said,
"Bye babes," to Sandra and closed the car door. He tapped
on the window, and I looked up and half smiled.

Sandra said, "Get in the front, I don't want to feel like a
chauffeur," so I did.

I didn't see Mano ever again after that night. Later, though,
I heard from Sandra that Mano had immigrated to Canada
and that she had received a postcard from Toronto of the
post office tower. He had ridden to the top of the tower,
which, he said, had made him think of her that night at the
tracking station.

MAGICIAN

There's a famous old calypso my mother used to play from the 1950s and the chorus went like this: *London is the place for me, London is a lovely city, you can go to France or America, India, Asia or Australia, but you must come back, to London city*. I was in Hampstead and this song was playing, when I found myself at a theatrical party, drunk on vodka and lemonade, and kissing a woman I had never met before. I don't quite know exactly how it happened, and it is the only time it has ever happened.

She wasn't pretty or beautiful, in fact she was plump and plain, and her turquoise satin trouser suit was way too tight. She also had hair under her armpits; I had never seen such thick hair growing there, like a small beard. She had asked where I was from and I told her that my family were from Trinidad, but that no, they weren't black. She thought that was strange. Then I told her that I was brought up in Yorkshire and she looked more confused. I told her my father was Irish and that he lived in Leeds, and she shook her dark head as though I wasn't making any sense at all. I thought, perhaps she hadn't heard what I'd said, so I leaned in to say it again, and that's when I breathed in her delicious and overwhelming perfume. Next thing, her hand was on the back of my neck and her mouth was on my mouth, her tongue moving back and forth inside it.

When my friend Della shouted my name from across the dark room, I pulled away from her and looked up. "I'll be back in a bit," I said, embarrassed, and made my way over to the makeshift bar, where Della, also drunk, was dancing.

When I was leaving, I saw the woman standing under the staircase; she was holding a man whose face I couldn't quite see in the half-light. I wanted to say something, to ask about her perfume, but it seemed rude to interrupt.

A few days later, I was passing through Old Compton Street in Soho, picking up flyers for a new play at the theatre where I worked part time. I was looking up at the Georgian houses, thinking how spectacular they were, and I was thinking about my job and how it might open some doors, when I remembered the magician, Marty St James, who had played at the theatre a couple of months before. He wasn't an ordinary magician; he was able to manifest birds, gold coins, and different coloured liquids. The night I saw his show, he pulled a snake from a woman's hair, made a young man levitate, and another disappear inside a silver box.

Della and I thought he was something else. He was pale, but his hair was almost black and so were his eyes. I remember saying, "If I could find a man like that, my worries would be over." And Della saying, "You and me both." On the last night of his two-week run, Marty St James gave me his card, and told me that he lived in Meard Street, in Soho, and that should I find myself in the area, be sure to drop by.

That day, when I rang his bell, he sounded both surprised and pleased on the intercom. He told me to come inside and make my way upstairs. The narrow hallway was dark and the walls were covered with large framed photographs of various shows. Some of the people in the photographs were South East Asian. Some looked American and glamorous. I wanted to look at the photographs more carefully, but I thought it might seem inappropriate, so I ran quickly up to the top of the stairs where I found him standing, wet and wrapped in a large white towel.

"My room is full of bubbles," he said. "Perhaps you can help me burst them."

It was true. There were hundreds of iridescent bubbles floating everywhere. "Oh God," I said. Then I tried to trap one in my hands and felt ridiculous when it floated upwards. I tried to catch another, and the same thing happened. "Come on," he said, "you can do better than that." Then, without thinking, I began to chase the bubbles, catching and popping as many as I could. The more I chased them, the more they seemed to rise. I noticed he was watching, smiling from a leather chair beside an enormous mirror; I caught sight of myself in my white, short dress.

Eventually, I sat down on the floor. Marty got up and stood in front of me. I looked down at his pale slim feet, and for some reason, I put my hands on them. Then I moved my hands up towards his knees, and then to the hem of his towel. I put my fingers underneath it, higher and higher until the towel came loose and dropped to the floor. I remember thinking, Jesus, what now. I had never done anything like this before. Marty bent down, took my hot face in his hands and said, "Stay."

On the floor, he stroked my hair and brushed his lips against my own, lightly passing them quickly, moving down towards my neck, and then my breasts where he stayed for a long time. Then his fingers began to play upon my flesh. I opened my eyes, and we were falling back onto his large, cool bed.

When I woke the room was dark. I lay beside him and listened to his breathing. Outside, I could hear a woman's voice; she was shouting. Then I heard a man shouting as well; they seemed to be having an argument. I was about to slip from the bed quietly, when Marty shifted the eiderdown and moved closer. With the movement of his body came a potent and familiar odour. He found my mouth and then he pressed his face into my neck and whispered, "You are a flower, and I am a bee." I thought that was a lovely thing to say. It also seemed to be somehow true.

For two days, we hardly left his bed. Sometimes we slept for a few hours, and then one of us woke and then the other woke. Now and again, he went downstairs and found something to eat in his luxurious modern kitchen. He brought me rye bread and soft cheese, apricots, chocolate, cornflakes, apples. Sometimes I heard him crying in his sleep, which was strange. I stroked his head and held him and didn't say anything about it. But I wondered what was wrong. Sometimes, when our bodies were exhausted, I tried to talk to him about his excellent show, his training, lovers he had known, or I asked about his family. Marty didn't seem to want to talk very much. Neither did he like to ask questions. He didn't even ask where I was from.

At the end of the first day, I decided to have a bath in his immaculate bathroom. There were bottles on the shelves, hundreds of bottles in different coloured glass. There were also bottles around the large tub, and some of them contained creams and lotions. I opened two or three before I found the perfume. Once again, I was overwhelmed. I dabbed some of the clear amber liquid on the tip of my finger and took the tiny bottle into the bedroom. Marty laughed and poured some of it into his cupped hand, and then he rubbed it into my back, legs, arms and neck. I said, "Is this magic?" and he said, "Of course. Everything is magic."

After three days, I remembered that I had a dinner date with Alan, my mother's ex-boyfriend. Alan had been ill, and he was in London for a couple of days seeing a specialist. We had made an arrangement to meet at a restaurant in Covent Garden more than two months before. Marty didn't want me to go. "I have to," I said, putting on my white dress; "this man has been good to me, and to my brother and my mother too. He might be dying." Marty made a joke and said if I left,

I couldn't come back. Then he suggested I call Alan at his hotel and invite him over to the house instead. "We can cook something for him here," he said. When he closed the door, I saw the rain had started. I clutched the bottle of scent and made my way to Covent Garden.

Alan was yellow and very thin. "I'm not as sick as I look," he said, and half smiled.

"You look fine," I said, feeling protective. When we walked into the restaurant he put his arm around my shoulder.

He'd booked a table next to a window, by diamond panes of green and lilac. I had never eaten at this restaurant before; it was sophisticated and filled with people who looked somehow important. Over dinner, we talked about his plans to move from his big house into a small, terraced house on the other side of the village. We also talked about my job at the theatre and Alan said it was terrific that I was working. I told him about the flat in Ladbroke Grove. He asked if I had a boyfriend and I said no, but I felt embarrassed and wondered if he could tell that I had just been with someone. Then Alan asked about my father.

"He has a woman called Ellen now," I said. "I think she wants to have a baby." I told Alan that my father sometimes telephoned and that he wrote twice a year, and always sent £10 at birthdays and Christmas.

Alan said, "Well that's something."

We were about to leave the restaurant when he reached across the table and picked up my hand. "Don't let go of your dreams," he said. "They're there to remind you of what's possible." He said this cliché in a serious way, and I didn't know why, but it made me feel sad. Then, he took out a camera and asked the waitress to take a photograph of us. I felt embarrassed, but I didn't say anything.

Eventually, he hailed me a cab, pressed some money into my hand and kissed me hurriedly on the cheek. I wondered if I would ever see him again.

★

The next day, I felt different, disorientated. I thought about telephoning Marty, but then I thought it might be better to wait. I walked to the supermarket and picked up some groceries, and then I rang the theatre and spoke to the manager. "Where've you been?" he said. Then, "Where are the flyers?"

I said I wasn't feeling well but that I would see him tomorrow. I spent the rest of the day lying on the floor next to the telephone.

When I telephoned Marty the following day, his machine told me he was unavailable. I rang his number every day for a week and each time no one answered. He must be away, I thought, on tour.

I was surprised by how much I wept when Alan died. The tears seemed to come from a place I had never visited before. My mother rang from Trinidad, and we spoke about things for a long time. She said she felt guilty. I said, "When it's over its over." And then I reminded her of the last few months before she left, when she was sleeping in the spare room, and they were arguing almost every day. Arguing in a vicious, unforgiving way. My mother said, "Yes, yes. I know." She said Luke was upset too, and I said, "I know, I've spoken to Luke."

Black days passed and then black weeks. I tried to carry on as before, but I could feel myself slipping into darkness. Sometimes, I thought, maybe this happens; you fall into a hole and you can't climb out and after a while the hole becomes familiar and you don't know that you're in it. Working at the theatre was difficult. When the manager suggested I take some time off, I was relieved.

In the flat, I thought about Marty. I thought about his bed. I swam in and out of fantasies – there to remind me of what's possible. I applied the perfume daily, on my wrists and my neck, and in strange way, I believed it was keeping me alive, like medicine. One afternoon, I walked down to the Portobello Road and found a record stall. I searched through boxes and found an old album with calypso tunes from the 1950s. I played the London track over and over. I wasn't sure that London was a lovely city, but I couldn't imagine being in any other place and feeling any different.

Della thought I should get away.

Eventually, she took me to Whitstable where we stayed for most of the summer with two lesbian friends of hers. I spent most of my time scribbling down my thoughts in a notebook, sitting on the pebbled beach where the wind was strong and cold. I think it brought me to my senses, the wind, the women, the regular hot meals. By the time I returned to London I felt like myself again.

A week later I was passing Marty's door on my way to the printers when I decided to call in. A woman came to the door. She asked if I wanted to see Marty. Then she said I looked very familiar. I wanted to speak but I couldn't. She leaned against the door with her hand on hip; the hair beneath her arms was thick. I said that I was sorry, that I must have the wrong house. I walked quickly to the other side of the street. Then I ran through Soho, weaving between tourists – there seemed to be so many of them – and business people going out for lunch. I almost crashed into a film crew on the corner of Shaftesbury Avenue and Charing Cross Road. Finally, I stopped to catch my breath outside the restaurant. I checked my purse and found there was enough.

The table by the window was gone, but once seated I was comfortable in the gallery. I ordered a glass of wine, and thought, this is a bad sign; you shouldn't be drinking in the middle of the day. Then I thought, who cares. The spring light poured through green and lilac diamonds.

DELLA

I didn't know what Della was going through. It wasn't something she talked about. Then one day when we were walking back from Soho, it started to rain heavily so we stepped inside the Photographer's gallery – an exhibition of Tina Modotti, the Italian activist and artist. Della hated the rain; said it made her feel worse. "Worse than what?" We were looking at black and white images of women and hands and roses. She told me about the darkness, a looming sense of dread she felt when she woke. It seemed to be getting worse; she couldn't shake it off; like wearing a heavy coat in the middle of summer. She said she thought I might understand.

When Della was eleven, her mother, Marianne, went upstairs to her bedroom and, wearing her nightie, lay down with the muzzle of a shotgun under her chin and fired through her jaw while the children played outside. I knew that Della was worried she might end up like her mother, that the agony was hereditary.

Some days, when I knew Della was struggling, I'd order her to put on trainers and shorts, and drive over the river to where I lived in Ladbroke Grove. We'd run around the Serpentine listening to Aretha Franklin or George Michael. We ran close enough to share music and headphones without getting tangled up. People said we looked the same, with our long limbs and blonde hair. At home, I made banana smoothies with mood-lifting, blue-green algae powder. We'd lie on my bed in pjs beneath the foot of the golden Buddha she'd painted years before and watch a movie. Sometimes, I persuaded her to go with me to a party in Notting Hill Gate. There were often people with money – directors, writers, models, the odd self-help guru. Sooner or later, someone would ask her, "What do you do?" While she tried to think of something to say, I'd watch Della's throat tighten up as if she was being choked. To say she was an artist felt like a lie, she said. But if she wasn't an artist, then what was she?

"You paint. You draw. What else can you be?"

"A fraud." She looked ashamed. "If I wasn't, I'd be selling my work. That's what a proper artist does."

"Then find somewhere for a small show. Something to aim for. It will help. You get to decide who you want to be."

Della found an exhibition space in Peckham. A reinforced concrete structure with a red-brick shell. "It will do," she said, showing me around the industrial building. "They used to make cricket bats here. It's cheap and it's light."

For the first time in months, I saw that she was hopeful.

During winter, when she wasn't at her day job, I'd find Della working in her rented studio. The soulless room came with an electric fire and a one-cup kettle. She played the radio and tacked photographs of her subjects on the walls. She wore her anorak and fingerless gloves, and I'd watch her mixing colours and smudging oils on large canvases, her cropped head bent over candy greens and reds. There was a painting of Marty and me. We were faint lines in avocado green. I was holding out my arms and he was a genie trapped inside a bottle. Sometimes I might bring a picnic, and we'd sit on the floor and eat; wash it all down with beer kept cold outside on the window ledge. I'd say, "Look, when you make your millions, you can take me to Acapulco; we'll drink margaritas with the Sierra Madre mountains behind us."

"Who knows," she said, "but if this show can lift me out of this funk, I'll be grateful."

★

At her private view, the evening sun shone through the long windows. Della wore a shimmery silver dress with a fluffy sweater on top. She put up her hair; she looked elegant, like an actor, like someone who knew who she was, but I noticed how thin and pale she looked. She was never without a cigarette. Guests were mostly family and friends, but her father had invited a couple of agents, and a gallerist from Barcelona. People he knew from his diplomatic life. I spotted them at once and gave Della a nod. They all seemed to want to be somewhere else.

The painting of me and Marty was the only piece that sold. The rest we loaded into a rented van when the exhibition was over and took it to her father's house in South London. We covered up the pieces with large sheets and hefted them up and into the attic. I wondered how she felt when I dropped her off that night.

Next morning, her voice was so weak and faint it frightened me. "I've got to get away," she said. "Got to."

We drove to a cottage in Somerset where hedges were high, and fields were bright and yellow with rapeseed. We stopped off at the market; "Strawberries or raspberries," I asked; then, "Brown bread or white?" She couldn't answer.

Every day, Della lay on an old rug in the garden. In between naps, she'd nibble on a salad or sandwich I'd prepared. Sometimes she walked around the yard, stared at the flowers or the fish in the cloudy pond. It wasn't until the end of the week that she started speaking again – about little things, like the climbing roses or the colour of mud when it dries on your feet, or how ginger beer can cool you down.

Maybe it's just a phase, I thought, as we drove back through the London suburbs.

Then Della lost her studio, and her beloved father died.

My landlord put the flat on the market, and rather than look for somewhere else to rent, I decided to pack up and go back to Trinidad for a while. Just a few weeks, I said. I needed to see my mother, see the hills at the back of her house, swim in the warm sea.

"Life is shit, and now you're going, too," Della said. "It can't get any shitter."

For three years we wrote letters and cards. I heard about Della's slow recovery, how, eventually, she started running a little more often. She told me about the studio she'd found closer to home, and her long days there working with waves and moonlight; the photography course she began; her recent exhibition where she sold more than half of her paintings. I heard about her new boyfriend, a curator for a gallery in East London. She had applied to the Royal College of Art to do a master's degree and passed the first interview. Fingers crossed for phase two.

When she called to say she wanted to visit, I hesitated. I wasn't sure I had it in me. For months, I'd felt darkness approaching, a broadening shadow creeping over my world. I had a sense of inertia, paralysis. I wasn't sure where I should be. London felt difficult, and yet, this place, this small island felt claustrophobic. At times this inertia was so bad I didn't want to get out of bed. I hoped it would pass, that I would find myself interested in things again – lunch, cinema, fashion, love. None of it mattered any more. Not a suntan or a night out or a job I might be good at. Della could not have known – my letters were upbeat, light-hearted as if by telling her, it would make the thing real.

"Maybe you should wait," I said. "It's hurricane season. Lots of rain."

"But I want to see you. It's been three years. Flights are cheap."

She unpacked her suitcase and told me about a five hour wait in Heathrow, and how a Nick Cave lookalike tried to chat her up in Barbados. I lay back, a pillow propping my heavy head. She looked different; her skin had a certain luminescence; her features were sharper, less round. Faint lines were around her eyes. Her hair was shorter, a fashionable cut with bangs.

"Not such a skinny binny, anymore," she said, patting her stomach. I smiled. It was true, she was heavier now.

"It suits you," I said, and I meant it. "You look terrific, Della."

She'd brought Mars bars and Tetley tea bags, ginger snaps and Jaffa cakes, a copy of *Vanity Fair*. She'd also brought a camera with a case full of lenses.

When we climbed down to the beach, Della said, "Look how white the sand is." She ran to the water's edge in her pink shorts and red T-shirt. "Those trees are amazing."

I told her that the trees were manchineel and if the sap gets on your skin it burns like acid. It can also cause blindness. The Amerindians used to put it on the tips of their arrows when they were at war.

"Oh," she said. "Incredible! I love that."

I followed her and watched her admire the leaves of the sea grape trees with their purple berries, how she marvelled at the burnt orange bark where light fell. I showed her the pool where the water was turquoise, and the rocks stood jagged and black.

I asked about her MA starting in September, the photography course.

"I love photography," she said; "it's really helped with my painting."

I noticed how bright her eyes were; how alive she seemed.

We drove through Canaan, and I was sorry about the heavy rain, but Della didn't seem to mind. She took pictures of the passing coconut trees through the raindrops on the windscreen.

"They'll be in focus and the rest will be blurred," she said. You'll see." She talked about depth of field, composition and circles of confusion.

Every day, she listened to me complain about the number of people on the beach and the loud music coming from the DJ under the trees. The thudding soca bass made me anxious. There were stalls selling all kinds of things: beaded bracelets, black coral totems, sugar cakes, tamarind balls, tie-dye wraps.

"It's getting like Camden," I said.

Della laughed. "Only so much better!"

She wanted to swim out to the boat where there were pelicans. I thought it too far, but she said let's try. That day, the sea was a metallic blue sheet, and the sun was low in a clear pale sky. After, we sat on the rocks and dried ourselves. Della said she was glad she'd come. "This is a kind of paradise," she said. "You're so lucky."

On her last day, we walked along the beach at the end of the runway. It was quiet there unless a plane was taking off or landing. The wind was picking up, and the water was choppy. The sand was grainy, and when the water pulled back, it exposed shells, many broken or chipped, and pieces of smooth green glass. My heart felt heavy as a sandbag.

"Do you ever still feel – you know – anxious? Remember when you used to get that choking feeling?"

She looked at me, smiled, then gulped in a comical way.

"Not so much."

I told her how hard things can seem sometimes; about the broadening shadow; about the mornings when I found it hard to leave my bed.

Della looked away at the sea. Then she said, "The thing is, you've got to keep going. Even when you're scared and sad, work hard. It's the only way. Work hard doing what you love. It's all in the detail," she said. "It's there for us to see. We just have to look for it."

She walked up the bank and stopped, held her camera to a conch shell.

"Come see," she said, leaning in, "with a macro lens."

I peered into the view finder.

The conch was frilly at the tip, and the whorl was old, pointy, white like bone. The flare of lip made the shape of a porcelain ear. The inside was flesh coloured, a deep pearly pink. I wondered about the meat of the mollusc – in Trinidad it was curried, served with rice. Not only was it a shell, but also an instrument. I remembered once hearing someone play a conch – a haunting, ghostly song. A miracle. I picked it up and held it to my lips. I blew. It made a faint, whistling sound. Like a call to something.

SAM

Sam and I went into the cinema. "We shouldn't be in here," I said, "we might see someone."

"Don't worry, Jews don't come here in the middle of the week."

"Where do they go?" I unwrapped my long scarf; the wind had blown my hair about; I took off my gloves and patted it down.

"Swiss Cottage or Hampstead. Town on a Saturday night."

I must have looked confused because he said, "Don't worry, you don't need to know about it." Then he walked across the foyer to where the ticket man was sitting behind a glass panel. The film had been running for a while, the ticket man said, but if we wanted to go in and see the end, as long as we paid full price we could sit where we liked – there were plenty of free seats. There was something in the man's eyes that seemed to say, *I wasn't born yesterday*. Sam slid his credit card under the glass. "You've made my wife very happy."

I pulled Sam by the hand and next thing we were running up the cinema steps. I was clinging onto the gold rail, and he was at the top, looking back at me as though I was a brightly coloured bird, something he had imagined or invented; something he was amazed by. I did what I always did when he looked at me in this way – I stopped right there and looked at him. Then I wondered what he really saw. One day I asked him, because he'd said, "You are the same now as you were on that first night."

I asked, "In what way?"

"I don't know," he said, "I really can't explain it." We were standing on the corner of a busy street, right there in Leicester Square, and it was very cold. People had to walk around us. "Beautiful," he said. "Seductive."

I said, "You can't put the two words together. Beauty is one thing – and beauty transcends sexuality." But even as I said it, I didn't know if it was true.

We found two seats at the back and in the corner. I couldn't remember much about the film except there was a ship tilted on the sea in a storm, and the music was loud, and I couldn't hear what he was saying. I remember his minted breath and thinking, *Don't do this*. I remember how his hand pressed my legs apart, how I angled my hips so he could find his way in, all the time thinking, *This is way too soon*. And then weeping at the end for no real reason at all.

When I'd first come to London, I'd taken a job in a small theatre. At the weekends, I had to open up the building before the show. If there wasn't a show, I would take Della there. This was when she was still a student at art college. She would sit in the lighting box and fool around with the switches and when I shouted "Lights!" the set – the clouds, or the forest or the inside of a house – suddenly looked alive, warm with yellow, or a cold, cold blue, a spooky green, or red like in a bloody thriller. If I didn't like the look, I'd say, "Change the lights!" Sometimes, I stood in the centre of the stage and did Desdemona before she dies, a burning Saint Joan, or Alice and the bit with the caterpillar, while Della followed me about with a bright spot.

We took to saying, when things were going wrong, "Change the lights!" That meant you had to look at something in a different way. For instance, if Della's grades were poor, she'd "change the lights," and instead of feeling unhappy, she might reassure herself by thinking that she had every chance of passing, and that's what mattered. Or if I went into town to buy a dress I'd been saving for and the dress was gone, I'd "change the lights" and think I'd find a nicer one. Of course, it wasn't always that easy to make some difficulties seem better, and sometimes we had to remind each other of this. If something really bad happened, you couldn't say, "Change the lights", like when Della's father had a blood clot and the doctor came into the Special Care Unit at St Mary's hospital and told her it was over. Della turned white, and someone brought a chair. I remember holding her hand, and thinking, *Christ, if you could really change the lights, it would all be very different.*

Sam and I had seen Della one night when she had just finished work. I said, "That's my friend, Della," and pointed through the window of the restaurant. We watched her cycle down the Strand, away from slow-moving cars towards the traffic lights, her fair hair blowing behind her like a pale banner, her reflective jacket shining in the twilight. I told him that she was a strong woman, and Sam said if she was a friend of mine, she'd have to be pretty special.

"Her father died, from a blood clot, last year. And look at her now," I said.

He was sorry to hear that; you never know what life would throw at you. Like his dad – just before the wedding – having a heart attack. They still didn't know if he was going to make it.

"Maybe that was a sign," I said.

"You could be right there."

After the cinema, we went to a Soho hotel. We drank hot chocolate in the reception room because we didn't want the concierge to think we were desperate. The room was small with dark wooden furniture; there were white sheets and white pillows on the four-poster bed. I had never slept in a four-poster bed before, and Sam said it was mahogany.

"I only like white," I said, my arms stretched above my head and my legs taut, as if I was about to dive from a high board.

He said, "That sounds like a race thing to me," and for a moment I thought he was serious and didn't know what to say. Then he smiled and said, "You're not in a hurry, are you?"

We kept the lights on, and I was okay with that. I was glad of the sheepskin rug on the floor, and glad that when I went into the bathroom I didn't look as pale or as tired as before.

"Don't go yet," I said, when Sam sat up and looked at his watch. I hooked my legs around his waist and said it again, but this time in my baby voice, which made him laugh, and he rolled back on the bed towards me, and we were very close, looking at each other, breathing in the same way.

It was strange waking up alone in a hotel room. I didn't bother with breakfast, just a cup of coffee while the bath filled.

I wanted Della to meet Sam, but she said she really wasn't up for that. She was too busy right now – maybe at the end of the summer. I said we could drop by one evening, but somehow it didn't seem to work out. Once we took a chance, but she was out. "I think she's left," I said, pressing the buzzer, again, in the dark street. "The thing is," I explained, "she doesn't like to hang around in town when she's finished working. She's like that, independent."

Sam said it didn't matter, maybe it was just as well, because Della sounded like a tough nut to crack, and probably he wouldn't be good enough.

When I told Sam about the time Della went to India on her own, he said, "God, whoever does that?" We were sitting in a restaurant overlooking the river and the sun was orange and going down. For some reason Sam wasn't wearing a suit that day, and his dark hair was away from his face. "You don't look like a husband," I said. "You look like a boy. A boy of twelve or thirteen."

"Good," he said, and reached across the table. "Does that mean you'll take care of me?"

"Maybe." I put my hand on his, and looked away at the glittery, orange water.

"Why does the idea of looking after me make you sad?"

"I don't know," I said. "I really don't know."

Then I told him about the things Della had made: the installation pieces for organised events and large-scale parties; about the transformation of the Battersea Power Station in the spring with huge bright flowers, butterflies as big as people, enormous birds flying through the scented air, giant rabbits jumping on mushroom-shaped trampolines. Della had a team of twelve making props for three months straight. Could you believe that? When I told him about the swimming pool she put in the park with fake fish and little coloured boats you could row, Sam said Della sounded like a "real pro". Then he said, "Maybe she can do something for us? Maybe she can make a little island that looks like Trinidad, with palm trees and blue water." I remember laughing, and then I told Sam that Trinidad wasn't like the other islands, that my mother's house was near a refinery and the sea nearby was dark blue, not how you imagine the Caribbean Sea to look. But my grandmother's house had been right by the best beach. You could walk down the road and in minutes wade into warm, clear water.

One Sunday, we parked around the back of the Kings Road and walked to the shops. Suddenly, we were looking at books in the basement of a large store. It was like that with Sam, one minute you were driving over the river in a silver car, and the next you were looking at Christ on the ceiling of a Greek Church, or samba dancing in the basement of some seedy club or having tea in a hotel lounge overlooking the park like a proper couple on a proper holiday. Sam said, "Let me buy you something," and I was about to say no but it was too late, he'd bought me a book of love poetry and written inside.

In a department store, we looked at shoes for his New York trip, but there was nothing he liked in his size. He bought two cotton shirts. I thought they were expensive, but he said you can't go wrong with that kind of cotton. We couldn't make up our minds about a jacket. There was something about leather jackets that I wasn't sure about, especially on men. Or leather trousers. Sam said he thought they looked okay on some people.

Even though it wasn't that warm in the restaurant garden, the sun was bright, so we could sit outside. The waiter said, "What can I get you?" Sam said, "I'd like some sparkling water, and my wife would like a glass of wine." I gave him a look, but he smiled, and I thought, *So what? Nobody here knows*.

I said, "I can't believe I'm seeing you at work tomorrow and I saw you today."

"That's how it should be," said Sam. "That's how it's going to be."

When I first met Sam, I failed to be aware of something necessary and unavoidable. I didn't know then he was about to get married, and I also didn't realise I was the sort of person who could be with someone who was married. Later, I thought, maybe that's the point. You find out things about yourself you didn't know and perhaps you shouldn't punish yourself for loving someone and not loving someone else the way you were supposed to. These were things I said to Sam when he was feeling particularly sad or guilty.

Like the time we were lying on the heath, and it was sunny and warm and we were making shapes from clouds. "There's Trinidad," I said, "like an apple core". Then, "a witch with a bent hat... Look – number eight." Sam didn't say anything. I pointed at two, high, well-proportioned clouds. "That's us.

We're moving in the same direction." Then I saw his eyes were closed, and I knew he wasn't thinking about clouds.

I soon realised you can only do this for a while. You can meet up, go to fancy restaurants, or a gallery somewhere and walk about looking at pictures and saying what you like and don't like. You can talk on the phone for hours about anything, because she's not there. While on the phone, you can eat dinner at the same time, watch the same TV channel or read from the same book (turn to page 101 and line 32 of a particular poem). But then something happens: a birthday comes, and you want to spend the day with the person, or you have some good news, and you want to call and say, *How about that?* Or you're lying in bed with a high fever, and you want his hand on your forehead; you want him to say, *You're burning up, sweetheart.* Or you want him to come to your brother's engagement party; baby-sit on Saturday night and pretend the little baby might be yours. And when someone asks, *How's your love life?* say, *Wonderful, he's coming over in a little while and you can see for yourself.*

And it's not that you are demanding, or difficult, it's just that you want to be able to do some of those things, at least some of the time. You imagine that one day you'll be able to do them. Then something happens, and you know why you can't. Like one Friday afternoon when a young woman walked up to my desk and said, "Is Sam here?" She was tall and dark, and I knew at once – because I had seen a photograph at the beginning – who she was. (In the photograph she was wearing a bikini and holding up a drink in a pineapple. It was a cocktail of some sort, and she was smiling, making a toast, perhaps, I don't know. And I remember thinking, what white teeth – like in a toothpaste ad. When Sam had said, "She's pretty," I said, "If she's so pretty, what are you doing with me?" Afterwards, I felt sorry I had said this, and put my head on the left side of his chest where I imagined his heart to be.) I pointed at the office on the far side and watched her walk across the room, her hips small in brown leather trousers, and open his door without knocking.

At home, I took the phone off the hook, opened a bottle of vodka and drank a full glass. Then I went to bed. When I woke it was still dark, so I got up and went into the living room and, for the first time in weeks, turned on the television. I lay on the sofa and looked at the ceiling, watching the flickering light. I drank some more vodka and went back to bed. By then the birds were making a lot of noise. I sat up and looked out of the window. The houses across the city seemed to me like huge graves pushing up from the earth.

Soon the neighbourhood would be waking up. I felt exhausted and wondered if I should take a couple of sleeping pills. I remember thinking, *This is how it happens: you feel unhappy so you have a drink or two. Then you take a few tablets and next thing you're lying in hospital with a tube down your throat and they're pumping out your stomach and trying to find out who and where are your next of kin*. I telephoned my mother in Trinidad, but there was no one home. Then I remembered she was away with Charlie in Caracas. I tried Luke.

"What is it?" he said, when he answered the phone; he was irritable, sleepy.

"Nothing," I said. "I just needed to speak to you."

He said, "Call me later, okay – in the morning. Try and get some sleep."

Della couldn't understand why I was so upset. She said, "What do you expect? You can't fall in a sewer and come out wearing a new dress."

On Sunday night, Sam turned up at the flat looking pale and scared. Even though I was sure it wasn't a good idea, I told him to come inside.

"I'm sorry," he said. "I'm really sorry." He sat on the sofa

and covered his face with his hands. He said he didn't know
what to do and everything was in an awful mess. His eyes
filled up as he talked. He didn't think he could cope any
more, he felt like driving off a cliff or throwing himself under
a train. For some reason I thought about my father. Why are
you so weak, I thought, and I stood and went over to the
window. Below, I could see his silver car, and two young
people under a streetlamp, leaning up against the wall. They
looked as if they were having an important conversation; the
boy, was kicking the base of a post and the girl was looking at
her fingernails. I remember thinking: All over the world, at
this moment, there are people doing the same thing.

I told Sam to sort himself out. I talked in a loud voice,
listing everything that was making me unhappy, and I
explained all the reasons why we could never work. I said
he was just too scared and that this was the end of the story.
I can't take care of you, I said, because you're not mine to
take care of. "What do you think it's like for me?" I said. "At
least you have someone to go home to." Finally, I put my
hands in the air and shouted, "Why the hell don't you say
something?" Then tears started pouring out of my eyes, and
he got up and pulled me to him. Soon I was crying so much
Sam said, "Hey, you're soaking my shirt. If you keep this
up, you'll have to lend me a blouse." The idea of Sam in a
blouse made me smile. I said, "How about a dress – you can
go home in a dress." Then, we both started laughing. Next
thing, we were naked and my legs were up and around his
back and he was moving swiftly. For the first time in many
months, it felt like we were actually going somewhere.

The summer passed slowly. I found another job, in Piccadilly,
and though the work was dull, somehow things felt easier.
Della wasn't around because she was working on a large
project in the City. In any case, she didn't have much time
for Sam. Whenever she called, she never asked how he was,

or if I had seen him. She didn't seem to think he was worth talking about.

I didn't see much of Sam. Sometimes, we met for a drink or a movie, but he always left early. He said it was important that he didn't make his wife suspicious; that way, he could ease out of his marriage without too much trouble. Now and again, he turned up on a weekend when she was out shopping, or having lunch with a friend. But he never stayed for long. Whenever I complained, he said, "Be patient. I'm going as fast as I can." I wanted to say, as fast as you can isn't fast enough for me, but I knew there was no point.

Once, when we were lying on my bed, I said, "Look, just stay here, and don't go back home. You can write her."

Sam said, "Why didn't I think of that?" So, we wrote his wife a short letter saying how sorry we were for causing her pain, and that we wished her every happiness the world could offer. Then we signed it and put it in an envelope. Sam said, "God if only things were that simple."

When Sam was there, I was mostly okay. But when I was alone, I felt myself slipping into a dark and fearful place where I couldn't stop thinking about his life with her. I wondered how they slept. And what they wore when they slept. And what they said to each other when they woke in the morning. Did they ever make love, even in a haphazard and unsuccessful way? Did they hold hands when they watched TV? What colour was their sofa? Did she ever run him a bath, and while he bathed, did she sit on the side and talk? Did she climb in the bath with him? Did he watch her put her make up on? Did she call herself Mrs. Goldman? Sometimes, I asked Sam these questions as a way of exorcising them, but I wasn't always sure that he told me the truth. Della said, "If he can lie to her, he can lie to you."

I knew that unless I had something to look forward to, or work towards, it would get worse. As Della said, it had been going on too long; nothing was about to change. Summer was nearly over. Did I want to spend another winter waiting? She said I should go away, somewhere warm, and think about things. "Change the Lights," Della said. "Go and swim in the sea, get out of this place for a while. "Go to Trinidad. Spend some time with your family." When I told Sam I was thinking about a break, he said, "That sounds like a good idea. We could leave after the Jewish holidays – when my wife is away on a business trip."

The travel agent gave me several brochures which I brought home and looked through. There were package holidays to various destinations in the Mediterranean: Greece (the islands), Morocco, and Turkey. There was a Caribbean break in Antigua which seemed to have all sorts of extras thrown in. Short breaks in Barcelona, Madrid, Antwerp and Venice. In France, there was an holistic hotel with Eastern practices. It had glass walls and ceilings and an enormous glass Buddha in the gardens. We could always take the train and go to Paris. I had only been to Paris once, a rushed trip, a fly-by-night on the way to somewhere else. Two weeks, or ten days. Or even a long weekend. There were all kinds of options.

    That evening we talked it over in a restaurant. I showed Sam the brochures and he said they looked really great. The only thing – he didn't want to go too far. It wasn't going to be easy, and – I must try to understand this – even if his wife was away, she would be phoning him at home. Where would he say he had been? How would he explain a suntan? I told him he was being ridiculous; nowhere was going to be that hot now. But what about his father, he said. It was very likely that his father would drop by one evening. And if his friends called and he was not there – where would they think he was? Tiredly, I got up from the table and said: If you don't come on this trip, I never want to see you again.

There were regular flights from Heathrow, and Sam had

made sure our tickets were flexible. That way, if for some reason one of us was late, we could get on the next available flight. I told him to pack sweaters and something waterproof because, according to the guidebook, it rained a lot in Dublin. Bring some walking boots too, I said. We might hire a car and drive into the Wicklow Hills. You don't have to go far to find countryside. I packed my book of poetry and remembered my bathing suit. It would probably be still warm enough to swim in the Irish Sea. We might even go horse riding out on the sand dunes. And if there was time, we might drive up the west coast and visit the town called Sligo, where I was born.

Sam said, "Slow down, we're only going for two days."

"Aren't you excited," I said.

He said, "Of course."

I waited for a while at the meeting point in Terminal One before making my way to the check-in desk to see if Sam was there. I was early and there was plenty of time. There were so many people I wondered if there was some kind of sporting event going on, or an Irish public holiday, but perhaps this was how it was every weekend. The woman behind the counter said it might be best to wait until my friend arrived before checking my bags onto the plane. I must have looked concerned because she said, "Don't worry, if the worst happens, you can change to a later flight." I found a place beside a pillar, sat on my suitcase and waited. I took out the book of love poems, but I couldn't read any of them. I read the inscription over and over and I thought, you don't call someone your beloved if they're not.

When the flight was called, I tried to reach Sam on his mobile phone, but the answering machine came on. That's the thing about trains, I thought, you can't get a signal unless you're travelling over-ground. There was no point phoning the office; he would have already left. A young couple watched my bags, while I found a kiosk and bought a bottle of water and a newspaper. They were going home after a fabulous holiday in London. They asked me where I was staying in Dublin, and I said I didn't know.

Two more flights were checked and boarded before I finally rang the office. The new girl answered the telephone. When I asked her what time Sam had left, she said Mr. Goldman was in a meeting.

I said, "What are you talking about?"

The girl said, "Would you like me to give him a message?"

I said, "You don't understand."

She said, "Is that you, Mrs. Goldman?"

Della said it would take time and there wasn't a quick fix. You just have to leave things alone for a while. In the meantime, she told me to cash in the tickets and go somewhere else. That night, she left work early, picked me up from the airport and drove me back to her house. We drank a bottle of tequila. Three or four quick shots with lime and salt, and the rest in tall glasses with ice and Coca Cola. Sometime after midnight, I looked out and saw the moon was like a big white plate. It was a warm late summer night, so we took a mattress and some covers outside, and under a clear sky fell asleep in Della's little garden.

In the morning, although I was tired and wanted more than anything to climb into a proper bed, I went with her to the City and spent most of the day tying streamers on the rail of the enormous ship she had built. It took a thousand yards of red and blue and gold ribbon. When the wind machine blew, it looked like it was moving.

CHARLIE

When I met my mother at the airport, I almost didn't recognise her. Her face looked the same, and yet, I knew something had happened, that she was somehow different. I slid her suitcase into the boot, made my way out of the carpark, then followed the complicated network of exit signs until, eventually, we found ourselves on the motorway heading north towards London. While I drove, my mother talked to me about the fires, the rising number of murders, the price of fresh butter in Trinidad. I wondered how long she would take to get to what had brought her here. It was a last-minute decision. A gift from Charlie.

The day before she left Trinidad, she'd had to rush around getting everything in order for him. She'd bought meat and packed it into the freezer. Stopped in at the store and picked up extra tins and other things – just in time, the village had already started to flood. She'd told Charlie he must buy fresh fruit and vegetables every now and then from the market. He had to take a basket and one-dollar bills because the stalls never seemed to have change. I looked at her and she admitted that he too had given her a look that said, Please don't worry about me you have enough to worry about. It had made her want to cry. "He's a good man," she said. "He's not perfect, but he's kind."

Another good thing about Charlie, my mother said, was that he didn't have a lazy bone in his body. He'd always carry out anything heavy from the car, like the two cases of beer and a case of Coca-Cola bought to last him while she was

away, though the past few weeks they had been drinking
more water than anything. He was generous, too. He used
to keep water in empty rum bottles that clanked about when
you opened the refrigerator door. She had replaced these
with plastic containers with plastic screw-on lids, though
she had thought them too expensive when they saw them in
the American store, but Charlie had said it didn't matter; if
she liked them then she should buy them. Sandra had said
how come my mother could get a man to spend money like
that. She'd bought the food for Charlie because in the early
days when he used to invite her for dinner, by the time he'd
finished cooking, she was so hungry she felt light-headed.
Usually, he made stew or a corned beef pie. But there was
never enough, so when she got back home to Sandra's
house, she made a sandwich and took it into Sandra's room.
Then they might play a silly game where Sandra would
try and guess what Charlie had cooked. Sandra was always
saying that Charlie didn't take my mother out enough. Get
him to take you somewhere nice and expensive. According
to Sandra, men were like dogs, and if you got them young
enough you could train them like you train a puppy. You
must teach the puppy to pee on the paper.

As we drove on in silence, I thought about what she'd told
me in her letters. She had written how she and Charlie had
started going into Port of Spain on Friday nights, and how
happy she felt sitting beside him while he drove. They didn't
speak very much, and she was relieved that they didn't feel
the need to. Instead, they listened to calypso tunes on the
radio and sometimes, if Charlie knew the words, he sang
along. He had a mild, clear voice and he made singing seem
easy. When she was with Charlie, she felt like she had come
home. It made her feel glad that she didn't have to go back
to a cold country where people didn't speak to one another.
    But if she said this to Sandra, Sandra would say she'd love

to have the chance to live in England. I knew my mother's response. "Oh, no," she would say, "England is all right for a holiday, but living there is another story." There were things that were easier in England, simple things, like walking to the local shop to pick up papers, or driving up the road to get petrol, but there were the layers she had to wear to keep warm in the winter, and how lonely England could be. No one seemed to know anything about Trinidad. They didn't know where it was. At the end of the summer holidays, when she came back all brown, someone in the Yorkshire village might ask, Are you back from Jamaica?

Sandra, though, loved England; it was the most beautiful place she had ever seen. When she was sixteen, she'd stayed with us – my mother, Alan, Luke and me – for six weeks. We took day trips to York and Liverpool, Wales and Scotland. We spent three days in London where Sandra bought clothes in the summer sales – fashionable summer clothes she could wear in Trinidad. She bought make up too, fancy clips for her hair, underwear. Sandra was happy and alive in a way I hadn't seen her before. My mother was only sorry that Alan didn't like her. He couldn't explain why, only that she made him feel uncomfortable. My mother said that was ridiculous and if he knew about her childhood, he would forgive her anything.

When she was a baby, Sandra's mother made her sleep in a dark, small room at the back of the house, made her eat meals alone in the kitchen. If people came to visit, she had to serve drinks and crudités, things she was not allowed to have. She had only two dresses: a dull, striped dress with a collar, or a plain shift dress that came just above the knee. If someone bought her something pretty, it was put away for special occasions that never came. She wore plastic flip-flops with rubber soles, her hair pushed back with a plain band. My mother had said it was wrong to treat a girl like that because some day it would all catch up and ruin her life.

Sandra needed looking after. So, every summer, when we rented the old house on the other island, she came to stay.

The house was near the sea. If you walked down the hill and cut through the long grass, you came to a small bank, and below was the beach. The sand was pale and smooth, though parts of the beach were rocky and crammed with coral bits, pebbles and broken shell. While my mother and Sandra would lie in the sun and tan, I'd walk along the beach for hours, looking for shells or pebbles we could take back home. I found bubble shells, music shells, white oval shells with a hole in the top like a tiny mouth, green shells with a silver glow, big conch shells you could put in the sun and bleach. I took some of them home but some I gave to Sandra to add to her collection, and she kept them in a tin. She said she would stick them on the base of a lamp, which she eventually did.

I remembered how, if my mother slept in the afternoon, Sandra would sometimes walk with me to the fort where there was a lookout with a flashing light and a wide view of the bay. Water was significant, Sandra said. Dreams of water, of the sea, for instance, told you about your emotions. Everything has a reason for being. Water, animals, air, dreams. Everything matters and yet nothing matters at the same time. Once she asked me what would happen if I lost my whole family, and I said I would probably die. Sandra said that wasn't good at all. She believed the most important thing was to be detached. Even if you lost your entire family in a terrible fire, you had to be able to come out the other side.

It was around this time that Sandra started reading esoteric books. Thinking back now, I can see that she was preparing for Shipper; that her soul was steering towards a metaphysical highway of meditation, reincarnation and gurus. From the fort we watched fishermen pulling in big nets of sparkling silvery fish and we waited for the green flash which, Sandra said, was a phenomenon without any scientific explanation. I remember looking into her large eyes and thinking that there was no getting away from it; she knew a lot of things.

My mother and Sandra had always been close, and I suspected that Sandra hadn't liked it when Charlie came on the scene. It went back to when my mother first returned to the island, after my grandfather's death, and didn't know what she was going to do. She knew that her relationship with Alan was over; that she wasn't going back to England. She knew she could stay with Sandra and Jimmy until she found a job and an apartment of her own. Sandra said there was no rush to do anything. She thought my mother should take it easy and settle in.

So, during the week while Sandra was at work, my mother did just that. She lay in the yard in the morning sun; or walked to the pool on the other side and swam for an hour or two. Swam in a way that was more like floating, thinking about her life and how it had changed. She wrote me letters at this time, one or two letters a week. She told me that freedom was frightening. That I should work hard so that I could be as independent as the man I might want to marry. She wrote how after lunch, she'd close the shutters and sleep beneath the fan until Loretta, Sandra's housekeeper, woke her for afternoon tea. She was very tired, she wrote. Thank God for Loretta.

On the weekends, my mother and Sandra drove all over the island seeing places my mother hadn't seen in years. She wrote how, during those long drives, the sun made all colours seem brighter – a Coca-Cola sign, a young boy's shirt, a bird or flower here and there – so much brighter than colours in England. While the warm breeze carried familiar smells of burning sugar or wood smoke or sea, she and Sandra talked about all kinds of things. Sometimes Sandra talked about her mother, how she wished she had been different and how she would never treat her children the way her mother had treated her. She confessed to my mother that before visitors arrived, she stuck the crudités in the dips, licked them and put them back on the plate; that she swilled rum punch around her mouth and spat it back into the serving jug.

Sandra talked about the holidays with us in the house on the other island. But most of the time she talked about her boyfriend, Jimmy, who ran a haulage business on the other side of town. He had been good to her at first, then something had changed. She wondered if she had made a mistake, having a child with a man like that. He was often away, and she didn't really know why. He never took her out or bought her anything new, though occasionally he came in with something for Joe, now three years old, or a bag of groceries, with her favourite things: wine, snacks, dips, chocolates.

My mother shared her deep thoughts and worries with Sandra, too. She told Sandra, that, perhaps, her bad luck with men had something to do with God punishing her for being promiscuous when she was young. She confided in Sandra about the abortion she had when she was sixteen (something I didn't know of until later), and, how at twenty-two weeks, the tiny baby clung on like it was glued to the wall of her womb. She cried when she told Sandra these secret things and Sandra seemed surprised to hear them.

Every afternoon, after she'd bathed and put on a clean dress, my mother made muffins or meringues, or a pancake mix in a box. She had tea with Sandra. Then they picked up Joe and drove down to the jetty where they played on the sand until the sun set. I knew this place well. Here, if the sky is clear, you can see the mountains of Venezuela.

Later, my mother had written about how she'd helped Charlie fix up his house. He said she had an eye. The house had been a mess back then. The walls were covered with green and white wallpaper – with a paisley velvet look, like something you might find in England. The wooden chairs were tatty, their varnish scraped; their orange cushions bobbled and worn. There were 1970's style plastic light shades hanging in every room, thick with dust. The kitchen was crowded with towers of containers from take-away restaurants. Every morning, while Charlie was out in the oil fields, she worked on his house. It was a good time to start because the dry season had just begun. She stripped and painted the walls, cleared the spare room and made new curtains and bedspreads. She fixed up the chairs with new covers; reorganised the kitchen with curtains and shelves. She filled baskets with ferns and hung them from the eaves, planted small palms along the driveway and orchids wherever she thought they might grow. I remember thinking, that's what my mother does; she meets a man, he falls in love, and she redecorates his house.

When the house was finished, Charlie said it looked like something out of a magazine. Sandra said it was beautiful and if only she could do something with her old place. Maybe she should start a bush fire in the yard, then claim on the insurance. My mother said she didn't need to start a fire; you don't need a whole lot of money to brighten up your house.

My mother wrote, too, how Sandra warned her to be careful. If things were made too easy for Charlie, he might not ask my mother to marry him. Why buy the cow when you're getting the milk free? My mother wasn't bothered about getting married, but she knew that Sandra was a romantic. I figured Sandra was jealous of Charlie; she said she wished Jimmy was more like him, she couldn't have found a more useless man if she'd placed an ad. My mother, she said, had landed on her feet.

Although my mother was sympathetic when Sandra complained about Jimmy, sometimes she wondered if Sandra

made things sound worse than they really were. She felt
uncomfortable when Sandra shouted at him for no particular
reason. Small things, like the way he parked the car, or left a
light on in the veranda, or dropped a towel on the floor, could
throw her into a terrific rage. Sandra might throw things, or
smash things like plates and glasses. Jimmy didn't say very
much; he went upstairs to sleep in the spare room. Or he got
in his car and went back up the road to the bar.

My mother had written once how Loretta had said, "Good
Lord have mercy, blood will spill in this house" and she'd
wondered if Loretta was surprised to see a white woman
behave like that. Once, when I rang from a telephone box in
Waterloo station and asked to speak with my mother, Loretta
said, "Your mother is a good woman, a good woman, you
hear," and then she hung up. I thought that was strange.

I'd heard how when Sandra had an argument with Jimmy,
she got depressed. When things were really bad, she stayed
all day in her room with the curtains closed. My mother
took her meals on a tray and sat by her bed and tried to make
her say something. Sandra would say she knew Jimmy didn't
love her, but she needed him in a way that wasn't good. She
felt like a trapped bird; she wished she could free herself up
and fly away to Europe. She could find a job in London and
live in an apartment overlooking the Thames. Then, when
she'd made enough money, she'd send for Joe. When Sandra
talked like this, my mother almost believed her. Sandra had
a way of talking that made you feel sure about things.

In the car that day, my mother told me how when Charlie
asked her to move in with him, it didn't come as a surprise.
He hoped it might be good for her and better for Sandra and
Jimmy, too, to have the house to themselves.

At first, my mother didn't want to tell Sandra because
Jimmy had disappeared again – he'd been gone for over a
week – and Sandra was angry. So, she waited for a couple of

days, until Sandra was calmer, and they were alone on the
jetty. The conversation went like this:

"Got something to tell you," my mother said.

Sandra said, "Let me guess. You're going back to England."

My mother said that was a ridiculous idea.

"You're pregnant."

"Sandra," my mother said. "Charlie asked me to move
in."

"That's wonderful news," Sandra said. "Aren't you the
lucky one?"

My mother said, "I was thinking, we could all go over to
the other island and rent the old house. You can bring Joe,
and we can take him to the beach. We can show him the
fort."

Sandra said that was a fabulous idea; if she got the time
off work, she would take Joe out of school and come. My
mother didn't know if she meant this, but Sandra was at
least trying to be enthusiastic.

The following morning, my mother decided to drop by
at Sandra's house to pick up some clothes. When she went
into the kitchen, she knew there was something wrong.
Glass was scattered across the floor, big chunks of glass from
a broken vase or bowl. The fan was thrown over and making
a rattling sound. Sandra had gotten into a rage. In the living
room, the curtains were still drawn, so she pulled them open
and saw a hill of books flung from the empty shelves, and
among them broken ornaments, papers, photographs, shells.
The shell lamp was smashed into tiny pieces.

Loretta was in the back room, sitting on her bed. When
she saw my mother, she got up at once.

"Miss Sandra went out."

When my mother asked where, Loretta began to cry.

"What is it, Loretta?"

She shook her head.

"Tell me, what is it?" Loretta sat at the kitchen table and

put her head in her hands. Then she said Miss Sandra would kill her if she heard her talking like this.

My mother said, "What do you mean? Talking like what?" There was a long silence before Loretta looked up.

"I want to tell you these things since so long, because I feel you are a good person. But I knew you would tell her and now it doesn't matter because you leaving here."

"What things? What things do you want to tell me."

Loretta said, "And if it don't come out today, it come out in a week, or a year, or in ten years. So better let it come out now."

"Let what come out now."

Loretta said, "She say you come in Mr Charlie's house and take it over like it's yours. How you make him spend money and take you to fancy restaurants. How you only looking for a ring to put on your finger."

"Loretta," my mother said. "You don't know what you're saying."

"And now he say to come live by him, she sorry for him because he don't know what he getting. She say you only bring sweet things like pancakes to make her fat; how you like to see her stick up in the house because you jealous; jealous of Joe. She say yu belly rotten like a rotten fruit – you go with plenty men. And if it wasn't for you, Jimmy might hang around but Jimmy know a whore when he see one. She say you kill a baby when you sixteen."

My mother said she couldn't remember going to the door or walking outside to the car. When Sandra passed her on the road, she said she wasn't feeling well and would speak to her later. She couldn't remember coming into the house, but Charlie said when he came home, she was sitting in the veranda staring out at the lake.

When Charlie saw how distraught my mother was, he had booked her ticket that same day. He called me and asked if I could meet her at the airport.

I said, "Of course! What a lovely surprise."

Then Charlie said, "While you're on the phone, maybe I can ask you something. I'd like to marry your mother. Would that be okay with you?"

ARNAUD

When Arnaud moved into the top floor apartment, he'd taken up the carpet and stripped and sanded the wooden floors. I'd often hear him walking up and down. Sometimes, in the early hours, I woke to the sound of footsteps above my bedroom. What was he doing at that time of night? I talked to Della; we speculated. He was trying out new shoes. He was counting steps. He was an insomniac.

There were four occupants in the Georgian converted house: Mrs. Weinschenk on the ground floor, a Polish woman in her nineties who barely left her front room; Johann Lesniak, a retired art historian. I was on the second floor and Arnaud was above. I liked Johann, but he was often bad tempered. It was Johann who complained about Arnaud slamming the front door.

"He's inconsiderate, selfish. Someone needs to tell him."

I said, "I don't even know what he looks like."

It usually fell to me to pick up the post from the doormat and file it in each pigeonhole. I noticed that Arnaud's mail came from all over the world – Turkey, America, Spain, Saudia Arabia. There were cards, postcards, letters, packages. His mail was by far the most interesting.

I first caught sight of him from my living room window. It was November; trees outside my window had lost their leaves, and I was thinking how I was dreading the winter, when I heard the front door bang, and there he was. Arnaud wore a long charcoal coat; he carried a leather bag. He looked like someone in a film. He glanced over his shoulder as if he sensed I was there. I stepped back from the window.

That same evening, I was trying to read, when I heard him clomping above me, back and forth, back and forth. Every time I reached the end of a page, I had to start again. I needed to finish a script before next day's work, but it was impossible to concentrate. What should I do? The local library was closed. I could go to Della's flat. I could pop to the chemist and buy some earplugs. But why should I leave my home to find some quiet?

I rapped on Arnaud's door.

He opened it at once.

"Mr Laurent," I said. "I live downstairs, and all I can hear are your shoes."

He ran his dark eyes over me, and I realised I was wearing the clothes I wore to bed – an old T-shirt, a pair of tatty cotton shorts, long socks.

"And please stop banging the front door."

He said something that sounded like an apology. I escaped down the stairs.

The following day, Arnaud slid a note under my door. "Sorry for the disturbances. Let me make it up to you. Please come for dinner at 7pm."

Arnaud had painted the living room walls a dark red. Lamps gave an amber glow. There were thick candles on the mantlepiece, a holy smell of frankincense. I liked the old green velvet sofa, a glass mid-century coffee table. There was a small antique dining table at the end of the living room with two chairs. The kitchen was immaculate, white shiny modern units. In his bedroom, there was a large bed covered with a ruby velvet eiderdown. On the floor, a suitcase full of clothes. There was nothing else. Although the apartment was tasteful, it felt empty, as if Arnaud could flee at any moment. What was there could be quickly packed up and shipped.

"It's a work in progress," he said. "I probably need a wardrobe."

I walked around tall columns of books about art, photography, travel. He said he never went anywhere without his books.

"I need shelves, too" he said, "and a rug." His mother had promised to ship a silk Hereke carpet. It should be here soon.

That night, we sat at the table and drank wine. Arnaud cooked a lamb and aubergine tagine, and pasta with citrusy sumac. Conversation was easy, steady. Arnaud told me that he was a journalist, an American citizen. He'd worked for the *Washington Post* as a correspondent in the Middle East. He loved Syria; and he admitted that his heart was still in Damascus. He had applied for a visa to return, but there'd been some difficulties and delays. It would take a few months to come through. In the meantime, he would carry on his research in the British Library. He was writing a book about modern paintings and politics in Syria. Pale, as if he had never seen the sun, there was a vulnerability about Arnaud that made me wonder if something bad had happened to him.

"Is Syria dangerous?"

"You must know where to go and where not to go. I think you would like it. And Aleppo. You can slip into a house and discover a courtyard with a fountain, and the most exquisite light."

He reached for a large coffee table book and leafed through the pages until he reached a section about Damascus. The images were vivid, atmospheric.

"In Damascus, you find men in uniform selling mulberry juice from silver trays. On the streets are carts of dried rosebuds, violets, dates. All kinds of wonderful things."

Arnaud didn't seem to want to talk about himself. Instead, he asked about my life. I wasn't used to it. How did I come to live in England? Tell me about your father? What books do you like? Where did you go to school? You have no one here except your brother? So where do you go when things are difficult? I explained that I had good friends.

"You're a resilient person."

I didn't feel resilient. The world was often frightening to me.

"You don't know me."

"I can tell."

He smiled, a warm and generous smile.

I told Arnaud, I wished I wasn't so sensitive. I felt everything too deeply.

"We are alive. Would you want it any other way?"

"My family live abroad. I hate goodbyes."

He seemed to understand. His mother lived in Istanbul; his father lived in New England. "Goodbyes are inevitable. It's best to do them quickly. No time to change your mind."

"Easier said than done."

"Maybe we should be grateful. Maybe when we part, we should say, thank you."

"Yes," I said, "that's a good way of looking at it."

I liked the way Arnaud listened, as if everything I said had meaning, as if the things I said mattered. I liked the way he looked at me. I felt a charge between us; something I hadn't felt in a while.

When I got up to leave it was midnight. I stood in the doorway.

"See you later, alligator," I said, immediately sorry for saying something so childish.

Arnaud kissed me lightly on both cheeks.

He said, "Do you know alligator's live to 100 years, which means there's a very good chance I will actually see you later."

Two days after, Arnaud caught me in the hallway, tired and frazzled.

"You look like someone who could eat a vegetable stew, some kibbeh and salad. And maybe a glass of extra cold Syrian beer."

Without hesitation, I showered, changed my clothes, and went upstairs to his apartment. The table was set; there was soft Bedouin music, a smell of garlic, onions, herbs. In the kitchen, Arnaud drew me towards him and gently kissed me. I felt the press of his warm hand on my lower back. I could smell his smoky, woody perfume. I thought, this is too soon. This is way too soon. After dinner, he led me towards his bedroom, and I raised my arms, and he took off my dress, and we fell onto his bed. He was tender, his touch deliberate, his fingertips slow and free and curious. I didn't feel self-conscious. I didn't think about myself. When it was over, I felt both empty and full. We looked at one another; we grinned. The ceiling was painted like the sky. I hadn't noticed it before.

Arnaud was gone for most of the day. Sometimes, he stayed in the library until late, but he was usually back in time for dinner. When I knew he was home, I went up to his apartment.

Over a cold beer, we spoke about our day, what we had for lunch, our journeys into different parts of London. I talked about the Spanish theatre company in residence, the flamboyant director from Barcelona. Arnaud had worked in theatre when he was at university. He had a solid understanding of drama, storytelling.

Those days, I barely cooked. I bought ready meals or picked up bits and pieces from the deli on Ledbury Road. But Arnaud cooked every day. He made delicious Arabic food. He baked flatbread, then stuffed it with beef and white cheese. He cooked sour cherry meatballs, and we washed it down with cold mint and orange water. He used pine nuts, pomegranates, lemons. He made nut cake with semolina and fragrant syrup.

We glugged Lebanese red wine in short-stemmed glasses. We drank Arak. In the months that I knew Arnaud, I had never eaten so well. By the end of winter, I protested.

"If I keep this up, I'll have to buy a whole new wardrobe."

"No, my darling. You must eat."

He complained that women didn't eat enough, that they were inhibited, self-conscious. It was no way to live. "Some of the women I see in London have no shape. They are sticks. Brainwashed to be skinny."

Once he brought me warm apple cake for breakfast.

"But cake for breakfast, Arnaud? It's not my birthday."

"Somewhere it is somebody's birthday. Eat!"

It seemed to me that Arnaud could do anything. When a button came off my blouse, it was Arnaud who sewed it back on.

"I am useless," I said, "I'll make a terrible wife."

Sometimes Arnaud sprinkled the bath with rose petals. He washed and combed my hair. He could recite Tennyson, Yeats.

I told Della I was experiencing a new feeling of both contentment and excitement – how did I not know of it before? All my relationships paled in comparison.

"It's so handy he lives upstairs."

I confessed to Della that this was just as well, as I never stayed the night. Arnaud couldn't sleep with someone else there. It was impossible, he'd said. In the early hours, I pattered down the steps and climbed into my own bed. Della thought this was strange. How can you get married if you can't sleep in the same bed. Who said anything about getting married, I said.

I called my mother; I spoke about Arnaud, about his voice, his unusual accent. This curious mix of French and American was fascinating to me. He was brought up in France. His mother was a ceramicist, and his father an architect. You will like him, I said. I've no doubt.

"You're in love."

"No, nothing like that. But I like him. I like him a lot."

I told her that Arnaud was waiting on his visa, and then he planned to return to Damascus.

"Well, be careful," she said. "You don't want your heart broken."

On Arnaud's mantelpiece there was a long, gilt-framed mirror, around which were photographs. His mother, his brothers, the house in Fontainebleau where he grew up. I caught him sometimes looking in the mirror at the two of us. I wondered what he was thinking.

I knew things had happened to Arnaud. There were signs. He was bothered by the smell of certain raw meats; fireworks made him anxious. One day, I came home from Portobello market carrying a watermelon. When I reached the landing, it slipped from my hands, bounced, exploded and splattered down the stairs and all over the walls. Arnaud dropped to the floor. Then he started to shake. We sat on the steps for a few minutes until he was able to steady himself.

"What is it, Arnaud? Please tell me." We walked slowly upstairs. He was breathing quickly, and I felt worried. I suggested we go inside to my apartment. He didn't want to.

"Just leave me for a while," he said, his head tucked up to his knees. "I'll be okay. Just go. Please go. I will be fine."

Once we drank too much wine. I smoked a cigarette out of the window. Arnaud put on some music, and we danced together before collapsing, drunk, on his bed at midnight. At 3am I was woken by whimpering, and I got up, disoriented. Arnaud was lying on the floor, pressed to the wall, as if someone had a rifle pointed at his back. I went to him and turned him over. His eyes were open, but he couldn't see me. I wanted to wake him; instead, I stroked his head. I said, softly, "It's alright. You're safe. You're safe, my beloved Arnaud."

In the morning, I told him what had happened. He didn't want to talk about it.

"Perhaps you should see someone? Speak to somebody?"

"Maybe." Arnaud got up and opened the window. "Come see, darling," he said. "Spring is definitely here."

Magnolia trees were in full blossom, goblets of pink and white flowers. I went to him; put my hands around his waist. Sunlight was pouring into the room. I felt as if we were blessed, and yet, there was something about Arnaud that I couldn't quite grasp. I wondered what it would take for him to open up.

One day, I asked him how he felt about me. This thing between us, what was it?

He said, "Do we need to know? Do we need to give it a name?"

"No," I said. "I just wish you'd talk to me."

"I do talk to you."

I found myself looking through his notebooks for clues. There were pages and pages of neat, tiny writing in pencil. Mostly he wrote about migration; he was examining how houses, homes and homeland are represented in contemporary global art, and in Middle Eastern art. When he caught me, he asked what I was doing. His voice was quiet, but his tone was sharp.

"I was just interested, that's all," I said, my cheeks burning. "I want to know what you're writing. You never say. You never talk about it."

We rarely went out together, and I was sorry about this. When I was invited to an event at work, or a dinner, Arnaud made an excuse. He was busy with research; he was expecting a phone call. We occasionally went to Kensington Park Gardens, and I linked my arm in his, and we walked around the fountain. We went to the cinema to see art house films. But it wasn't often. Della encouraged me to bring him to her house for supper. He refused. Arnaud admitted that he didn't enjoy socialising; he liked his own company; he liked my company. He didn't want to hang out with strangers. I told him, they were strangers before, but they wouldn't always be. That was the whole point of meeting people. No, he said, he would rather be alone. I began to feel resentful. What was the point of having a boyfriend if you never went out? I wanted to go away with him. We could take a ferry to Ireland. I could show him the town where I was born. Had he been to Ireland?

One night, there was a high-profile premiere at the theatre. I asked Arnaud to come and meet me. Dressed in a long turquoise Alexander McQueen satin gown, I chatted in the foyer to producers, writers, and press, all the while looking everywhere for Arnaud. By the time I reached home, heady from too much champagne, I was angry.

"Is it so difficult to come to a premiere? It's hardly the worst invitation. This was an important night for me. You like theatre. What's the big deal?"

I told him I was sick of staying home. I felt like a prisoner. What about his friends? What about his family? I would like to meet his mother, I said. Did she know about me? Was she even real?

Also, I wanted to stay the entire night in his apartment. I didn't want to go back downstairs to my flat. Why couldn't I stay there? Why couldn't we sleep in the same bed? I wanted to wake up with him, and for him to be the first person I see. Arnaud said it was impossible. He must sleep alone.

I blurted, "How can we live together if we can't even sleep in the same bed?"

Arnaud looked taken aback. He told me that perhaps he had miscalculated. Perhaps he had misled me. "Perhaps we should take some time off."

He left me alone in his living room. Eventually, I went downstairs.

I let days pass. I got up and went to work at the theatre.

An opera company had moved in and started rehearsals. During lunch, I sat at the back of the theatre. When I heard the soprano, full of longing and pain, I began to cry and cry. I realised that I had started building dreams of a future with Arnaud. I'd assumed he was thinking the same. How had I got it so wrong?

I decided to avoid him. I didn't want to hear his footsteps. I didn't want to know when he was home. I decided to spend the weekend with Della. On my way out, I saw Johann. He asked if I was okay.

"Is it your selfish boyfriend?" He pointed upstairs. "Has he hurt you? Let me punch out his lights."

When the courier rang the bell, I signed for the package on Arnaud's behalf. I saw it was from the Syrian embassy, and instead of putting it in Arnaud's pigeon-hole, I waited until I knew he was home. I dressed in a new black blouse, my favourite jeans. I wore the perfume I knew he liked, and I put up my hair.

He opened the door; his face was lit, and I saw that he had missed me. We held one another for a few minutes. I breathed in his scent.

He looked at me intently for a moment, his dark eyes alert and alive.

"Everything okay?"

"Yes," I said.

Arnaud made tea, and we sat at his dining table. The package on the table sat between us like a grenade. I told him about the opera opening next week. He said he would like to come and see it.

"I love opera. My mother used to take me when I was a child."

"Go on," I said, "open it."

His American passport was inside; the visa had been approved. Now he could return to Damascus.

"Let me come with you," I said, half joking. "I can carry your books."

While I prepared myself to say goodbye, Arnaud was caught up arranging transport, medical insurance, finance, his international driving license. Each evening, I cooked dinner in my kitchen, and we pretended that nothing between us had changed. I made Trinidadian dishes; I cooked pelau, salt fish cakes, and fried plantain. We drank rum punch. Arnaud said I had deliberately hidden my culinary skills, and now he felt duped. I laughed. Della said it didn't have to end, just because he was going away for a bit. But I knew it was over.

That afternoon, I came home early from work. Outside, the sky was dull, a greyish white. Trees had lost their leaves. I turned on the television and made a hot drink. I waited to hear Arnaud come in the front door. I listened for his footsteps, and I eventually went upstairs to his apartment. The door was off the latch. The apartment was empty. Everything had gone.

Three months later, a postcard arrived from Syria. In Arnaud's neat handwriting, I read, Thank you.

ANN

Ann Sanchez took me to the store in Rosa's old car with electric windows. The power had gone so it was dark inside. I bought some cigarettes, a paper, a packet of sugar-free gum, and two club sodas, one of which I opened immediately. Ann said water with fizz is no good, and drank some anyway. Outside the sky was huge and bright blue. A plane flew so low I thought it might hit the tall refinery pipe with the violet flame.

"They're spraying again," I said, as we made our way to the car. "Sometimes they fly above the house making a loud grating noise, over and over, until I feel like screaming."

"You shouldn't get worked up about these things; after a while it shows on your face." She turned and looked at me, her dark eyes squinting in the glare. I asked her if I looked older. The last time she'd seen me had been in London, at the Commonwealth Institute. Sam had dropped me off just as Ann arrived.

"You're not that old," she said, and smiled. "And what does it matter anyway. Look at me. I'm starting all over." She laughed, and I thought of a pony called Twinkle that Alan nearly bought me when I was a child. It was a small grey Shetland pony. They had always seemed large, Ann's teeth, and yet for some reason, that day, they looked more pronounced. I wondered if it was because she had lost weight. I was thinking this when she jiggled the car keys and said, "Let's hit the road in Rosa's dodgy Datsun."

My door wouldn't open, so, as before, I had to climb in through the back and stretch over into the front seat.

"I want to know how you got so thin," I said, feeling self-conscious when my right hip stuck on one of the seats. Sometimes, when I walked, I felt sensual in my new heaviness, but when I saw a woman like Anne wearing tiny clothes with her stomach free and flat, I felt like one of the big American-looking women I sometimes saw in the shopping mall. Ann said it was her little secret.

She sang two songs on the way to the club, one about love, then an old one I recognised about leaving on a jet plane. She turned on the radio and seemed happy to hear Dolly Parton singing "Nine to Five". She moved her shoulders up and down to the beat and mouthed the words as though she meant them. Outside, the sky was filling up with puffy white clouds, covering up the blue and the sun. I wondered where my life was going and wanted to cry.

"If I'd known things were going to be this hard, I would never have come."

"Come where?"

"To this world," I said, tears were now filling in my eyes.

Ann said she wanted none of that. In a minute I'd have her going too. "There's a whole world out there, full of all kinds of possibilities. You can't waste your time feeling sorry for yourself. You've got to get on." She was getting so excited, wagging her finger, that the car was swerving, and I thought she might hit one of the casuarina trees, or the sloping bank.

When we stopped, she opened up the glove compartment and pointed to a flowery box of Kleenex. Beneath it was an old newspaper-clipping showing her mother modelling a crocheted dress.

"I never knew she was so beautiful," I said, wiping my nose. Ann said she wished she could have looked like her instead of like a horse. I thought, you mean a pony, and Twinkle came cantering back. She'd found the clipping in a trunk at the beach house and had taken it from there. Her mother would have died if she'd known her husband had kept it for twenty-five years.

It was the first time Ann had mentioned her father since the funeral. We weren't surprised when he died; it had been coming for a long time. Dr Sanchez was a proper West Indian gentleman. He wore long pants, long-sleeved shirts and shiny lace-up shoes – and always smelled of cigarettes. I used to think it strange for a doctor to smoke like that. When he got emphysema, he had to stay at home with an oxygen tank and a full-time nurse.

Ann was his favourite of the three. I knew her world had circled his. She said she'd never married because she couldn't find a man as nice as Papa. She worried about him, but I knew he had worried about her more. He told me once she might drift through life and end up with nothing – no husband, no home, no children. But she's an artist, a musician, I'd said that day; she needs to feel free. She'd come back just in time – the day her plane landed was the day he died.

I'd felt sorrow seeing Ann on the morning of the funeral, standing by the church door in her black suit, her two pretty sisters beside her. I'd never seen them all together before. They didn't come back as often as she did. They had English homes, English husbands and they went to Greece or Spain for their holidays. Ann still lived with her mother in a big old house in Camden Town.

On the day of his funeral, Ann had greeted me with a smile that seemed to say, *Thank you for coming but I wish this wasn't happening*. The church was full, and the coffin was open. I didn't look, but my mother said his skin was grey and waxy. I cried when our neighbour sang "Ava Maria". Then Ann gave the eulogy in a steady voice without a single break. I glanced over at her now and then throughout the service and was surprised at how strong she seemed. Outside, when everything was over and I saw her smiling, with her arm around Rosa, I remember thinking how pleased her father would have been.

Seeing her so bright and cheerful in Rosa's car, I couldn't believe it had only been two weeks. I thought she'd have been in bits.

Nobody was by the pool, so we could take our pick of where to sit. I lay by the small diving board, near to the table where we put our bags. I remembered finding Ann's necklace, and how it brought us together. I was quietly proud of our friendship. Ann sat beneath the stripy shade, covered in cream, looking at an English magazine. I had just closed my eyes when she said, "You might get cancer if you're not careful. You might even have it already." Then she came over and bent right down by my face to show me pictures of four 30-year-old women taken with a special camera to show sun damage. One looked like fifty, but I thought the others were okay, and what did it matter if no one could tell in real life. I rolled over and pulled out my notebook from beneath the towel. The pen was trapped between the pages and the green barrel was hot. I imagined the ink bubbling inside.

Ann sat by the edge of the pool and let her legs dangle in the water. She said she was glad she lived in a cold country, where you couldn't get sunburn and dengue fever and didn't need to have a car to go anywhere.

"This place is getting dangerous." She asked me if I'd seen the news last night. Two women got chopped and a four-year-old was raped and killed.

"It's not just Trinidad. Anywhere is like that these days. Pick up a paper in New York or London and you'll find the same thing."

Ann said it was because of unemployment. That's why she liked being in England where there were better job opportunities. When she got back, she was going to apply for a job with Marks and Spencer. She'd get a pension plan, medical insurance and paid holidays. Then she'd be secure and maybe one day she'd buy her own place, near the river, with a view of the park. She was fanning herself with the magazine, talking in a loud and unfamiliar voice. I sat up.

"What about your music?"

"Music doesn't earn money, and money makes the world go around." She made a swirly pattern in the air with her finger.

"You can't stop playing, Ann. You always said you'd die without it. From when we were young, right here, sitting by this same pool."

Ann made a face and said that was then. Then she pushed back her short hair and asked if I'd noticed how shiny it was. It was a special shampoo that you couldn't buy in Trinidad. "It's very expensive. Smells of apples."

She was standing, her face like a clown where the cream had run. I noticed how bony her hips were; her hands rested above them, ring-less and thin. I remembered her first concert in Port of Spain more than ten years ago. Her figure had been fuller then, her hair frizzy and long. That night I saw her take her father's hand as she wandered through the crowd. She wore a blue silky dress. I'd never seen her so happy; Rosa was out of the country on a sabbatical.

"You know my sister Lou runs the Baker Street branch – at least the food department. She said she could get me a job – just like that." Ann snapped her fingers. "And it's not far from Camden. They have training courses, where you learn about customer relations. I'll get discount too. Sometimes Lou brings home free cakes and pies when the sell-by-date runs out."

"Great."

"They have a management scheme so you can climb the ladder. You don't have to be a cashier all your life."

I didn't know what to say to that, so I didn't say anything. The sun was overhead and sweat from my forehead dripped

on the page where I'd written the word "green". I ran through
the alphabet and got "lean" and "mean" and "queen". Ann
wanted to know what I was writing. Some silly poetry, I said.

At the snack bar, we bought fries because it was all they had.
I covered mine in yellow, red and white stripes. She said
I shouldn't eat mayonnaise or ketchup, and fries weren't
good, though better than burgers or nothing at all, and then
threw most of hers in the wire bin. I remember thinking,
What's the point?

I jumped into the cool water and swam to the other side,
cutting through the pool with curved hands. She met me at
the shallow end where the steps were. While we bobbed in
the water like the old people did, I said wouldn't it be nice
to be a fish. Ann said she'd rather be a bird and looked up at
the clear blue sky.

I lay on my front to bake my back. I imagined the water
rising up and spilling over the sides of the pool, swilling
and flowing over the hot concrete, finding my fingers
first, lapping over my right side, washing over my legs. I
thought of the cold and the world I'd left behind. I thought
about Della. She would have liked to be there, too, by the
swimming pool. I wondered if Della and Ann would have
much to say to one another.

Ann was reading the paper. I could see her making circles
with alternate feet. She saw me looking at her.

"You have to do this when you're getting older, to keep
the circulation going. You might think you're young, but in
no time, you'll be my age, and then what will you do."

"Come and live with you. When you have your big fat
pension from Marks and Spencer." I laughed and looked up.
She put down the paper and glared at me.

"There's nothing for me here, you know." Her voice was
gravelly and cold. I sat up and felt the dizzying effect of the
heat. Then, I got up and slowly walked towards her.

"Ann."

Her eyes were burning, and her hands gripped the sides of the chair. "I'm not like you." She said it as if she hated me.

She was standing now, leaning towards me; trembling. For a moment I felt afraid.

"Ann, you said yourself this is a new beginning for you." I reached for her shoulders to steady her, but she pushed my hands away.

"He went out like a little flame. Puff." She clicked her fingers. "One minute you're here, next you're gone." Her nostrils were flared and her face was flushed. I moved closer, just inches away from her. I tried to steady my voice.

"You have your sisters, Ann, you have your mother, your new life…"

"It's over. Trinidad is over." Her face crumpled like tissue, and she began to cry.

I pulled her close, and when she tried to break away, I held her firmly in my arms and softly told her, "Let it all go, Annie. It's going to be alright."

We stayed there like that for a long time, Ann sobbing like a child, me holding her, and wondering why life had to be so hard. Some young people passed around the table and looked at us, but I didn't care. I could feel her thin back and smell the apples in her hair.

THE WOMAN

Helena said the mango tree was bearing and I said maybe
we could fill a bucket, make chow or chutney. It had been
a long time since I'd eaten chow. I wondered if we should
take the car, but Helena said no, a walk would stretch her
old bones.

I said, "There's nothing old about you, Helena." But
I could see the difference in her this trip. Beneath her
headscarf, her braids were white, and her skin was looser;
her legs more bowed than straight.

We set off up the hill just as the sky was starting to soften.
I offered her my arm. I liked the long hill, and the smooth
road leading off it. There were houses along here, some
hidden by trees, some tucked away behind hedges; their
verandas looked out on the lake. In the distance, I could see
the silver lights of the refinery. I was leaving in a few days
and feeling nostalgic.

Ahead, a dog barked and barked. I knew Helena was
cautious about dogs, and I was glad the dog was tied.

I said, "Look, that dog is like Buddy, remember Buddy?"

Half Pomeranian, ginger and toothy, my grandmother
adored Buddy. He trailed behind her in the house, hopped
into her car when she went to the grocery. You'd see Buddy
on the front seat of her red Hillman, nose up, ears pert.

"Lord, yes," Helena said, and shook her head. "How I
could forget."

I reminded Helena of how Buddy protested when
my grandfather came home from the refinery, as if my

grandfather was an intruder. He'd say something like, "That blasted dog", or "Damn that dog."

"Buddy know what your grandfather was." Then she said, "Your grandfather was a cruel man."

I knew that Helena had never much liked my grandfather, while to my grandmother she was intensely loyal. I'd heard her call him a devil but didn't know why. I suspected she had seen and heard things – like when he had said something racist about my friend Ann. As we walked the long road, and cicadas clacked like castanets, she told me something I would never forget; something that would change my perspective on my grandfather forever.

I knew how when he came home from the refinery, he'd wash off the stench of sweat, sulphur and oil, and put on his home clothes. But once a month, Helena told me, he shaved for the second time that day, dressed in a fresh starched shirt and pressed, dark slacks, slicked back his black hair with bay rum and splashed his face with Old Spice. "On his way out, he check himself in the long mirror," Helena said. He was good looking. My grandfather's eyes were dark and deep set. His frame was big, his hands were strong.

While this was going on, my grandmother was in the kitchen, or in her sewing room, or on the telephone. He might say goodbye, or he might not say anything at all.

"She smell his cologne and she know. He reverse out the driveway in his blue Chevrolet like a star boy, a lover man, cigarette in his mouth, window down and elbow out the car."

Back then, it took about an hour and a half to reach Port of Spain. Helena knew this because her family lived in Laventille. At Queen's College, he'd take a left turn and make his way to St Clair and to Mary Street, and the colonial-styled house where the American woman lived.

Helena knew about my grandfather's visits because Ida, her sister, was employed by the woman. Like Helena, Ida wore a green gingham dress with a green apron and a matching hat. Helena said Ida was a hard worker, but the woman didn't seem to think so.

"Ida say how you grandfather skip up the steps. Music always playing in the house. She like opera. If you call that music."

I tried to imagine my grandfather entering this woman's house with music playing. I'd always thought he didn't care for music. He complained when my grandmother listened to the radio. Maybe he was moved by opera. When I suggested this, Helena said, "Nothing move your grandfather. Not music, not God. How many times I must tell you?"

Helena told me, too, that my grandfather, who never cared for plants, who never bought my grandmother flowers, bought this woman many orchids and the woman spent hours with them in an atrium, misting them, pulling away old blooms and dead stalks. I had never liked orchids, with their spindly bright flowers, their thick leaves like plastic. I knew my grandmother didn't like them either.

"She have nothing better to do. No chilren, no husband, no chores," Helena said.

The woman would shout for Ida to make drinks, and Ida had to make whisky sours for them, just like the woman had shown her. Ida would take the drinks to where they sat in the back porch, away from the eyes of the world. Here, Helena said, my grandfather embraced the woman and kissed her on the lips, even while Ida was there.

I felt uncomfortable when Helena was talking about it, as if this was something I shouldn't know. There were jokes about my grandfather over the years; he was a ladies' man, a Romeo. I knew my grandmother had been unhappy, but I hadn't known why.

I asked Helena if the woman was beautiful.

"Never. She thin and scrawly and ugly; the opposite of you grandmother."

Once it was dark, Helena said, they came inside and settled in the drawing room. The woman worried someone might see them – people often walked by and peered inside. So the woman bought long curtains, sheer enough for a breeze, thick enough for privacy.

Ida told her how my grandfather sat in the planter's chair, or they sat together on the chaise longue. They talked about the woman's husband's hotel in Independence Square, worries over land in Martinique, her mother's flat in Paris. They talked in front of Ida as if she wasn't there. My grandfather listened, threw in his ten cents, things he said he'd heard at Country Club.

"He didn't like Country Club," I said. "He never felt he belonged."

"He didn't belong there," Helena said, "nor at Mary Street nor at Country Club nor the work Christmas party, nor family dinners. He didn't belong in his own house. Because he belong in hell."

Around seven, Ida had to bring them snacks, but she knew my grandfather didn't come there to eat, and after a while, when my grandfather gave the woman a knowing look, Ida was dismissed.

"That woman like sex," Helena said. "Anywhere and anyhow. That is the kind of woman she is. A loose woman. A jagabat."

The thought of my grandfather and this woman together made me feel strange, queasy.

By now the light was low as we climbed the hill, and I could see the bamboo twitching and dark. I remembered my mother telling me that bamboo was full of tarantulas.

"Did my grandmother know he was having an affair?"

"She knew something, but she didn't know who."

Helena said my grandmother asked my grandfather about his visits to town, but he didn't answer. She overheard my grandmother crying on the telephone to her sister. She heard her praying; praying the holy light of God might fall on my grandfather, that he might see what he was doing to her. She telephoned a healer in New York, and another in Florida. She saw an obeah woman in Gasparilla who told her to let the thing play out. On the nights that he was gone, she'd call Helena to bring her an extra dose of Valium. By the time, my grandfather came home, she was asleep with Buddy curled up at the foot of her bed.

At breakfast, my grandfather ignored her. He ate his breakfast, drank his coffee and left for work.

"I tell her, I say Madam, don't cry. All men is the same. Only some worse than others."

I thought about the men I had known; I didn't believe they were the same.

Helena carried on. Her voice was steady and even, as if everything she was saying had been held inside her and now it was allowed to come out.

One time when he was visiting the woman, trouble was brewing in Trinidad. I had a memory of this. I recalled my mother talking about an uprising, a surge in violence, an army mutiny, white people running away to Miami and England. In Woodford Square, an official's car was turned on its back, then kicked and battered and set alight. Thousands of people marched from Port of Spain to Caroni in protest; there was a demonstration in Frederick Street, and crowds stormed the cathedral.

Helena described how, one evening, my grandfather arrived at the woman's house as usual, and he was in a good mood. Ida came in with a tray of drinks and nuts. The woman told him she'd been shopping in Frederick Street and a crowd was outside a shopfront and a man was speaking through a megaphone, saying, *They using white mannequins to sell clothes to Black people. What kind of foolishness is this? Who these people think they are? These people real dumb. They think we dumb too.* The woman turned to Ida and said, "You believe in that nonsense? Why you people angry? Why you people so ungrateful? What more you people want from us? Haven't we done enough?"

My grandfather said there was a lot of talk going on, a lot of scaremongering. He said they should relax, forget about all this for now. He put his arms around the woman. The woman agreed, drew the curtains and sat down beside him. She told Ida she didn't want to see her again that evening. She said it in a mean way, as if the unrest was somehow Ida's fault.

Then the woman put on the gramophone and turned up the volume. From outside, Ida heard what sounded like the banging of drums. She went into the drawing room to tell the woman, but the woman and my grandfather were embracing.

"Ida run upstairs and look at the crowd at the top of Mary Street," Helena said.

The crowd were chanting and moving down the street, and the leader up front was dressed in African clothes, and he was holding up his fist. Ida said she thought it was likely the same leader the woman had seen in Frederick Street.

Then the woman and my grandfather came upstairs. They asked Ida what the hell was happening. They opened the window to hear, and the woman yelled at my grandfather to step away, keep out of sight.

The crowd was moving quickly, shouting *Black power coming! Black power now!* Some were carrying sticks and metal dustbin lids. Some broke free and were running towards the houses.

Ida saw people jumping over the gate. She, the woman and my grandfather ran downstairs. Then someone pitched a bottle at the front of the house and smashed the drawing room window. Flames caught the long white curtains. Soon the whole room was on fire.

"The woman frighten," Helena said. "She shout at Ida.

Tell them to go! Tell them! They will listen to you! The woman shake her shoulders. *Tell them go away! They hate us!* Then the woman try to push Ida into the burning room to save the paintings."

Ida fled to the back of the house.

Outside, there was loud chanting, clanging of spoons on bottles. From a distance came the whirr of sirens. The woman and my grandfather ran out into the atrium and squatted down under the orchids. But then they realised they could burn alive, there, too. They ran down the outside steps and climbed inside the back of the Chevrolet.

Ida told Helena how the police arrived with basket shields and riot staff, and they shot their guns into the night sky: *pop, pop, pop*. The crowd broke and spread out. The fire was bright and raging at the front of the house. Then the fire brigade arrived, and they started hosing down the place. Ida stood on the side of the road and watched. She didn't want to go back inside the house.

When a Black Maria pulled up, my grandfather and the woman stepped out of the car. Ida heard an officer say, "Sir, is this your wife?" The woman said, "He's just a visitor."

When my grandfather came home, Helena said he looked as if he had come back from a war. His hair was dishevelled; his shirt black from the fire. He didn't say anything to her about the way he looked. In the morning, my grandmother asked where he had been, what had happened to him. Was it something at the refinery? Did something happen? An explosion?

My grandfather said, Yes, something happened. But he didn't say what. It was Ida who told Helena, and Helena then told my mother. And now Helena had told me.

I remembered more of what I'd heard about the curfew, how there were rumours that things were about to get worse. Black Power was real. The prime minister was nowhere to be seen; the country was in a state of emergency. But the refinery camp was protected with security guards at both entrances, and this was reinforced with soldiers from the army. Once people were vigilant, and once they obeyed the curfew, my grandfather said, they should be safe enough.

That day, Helena went with my grandmother to the grocery. They bought goods to see them through the next three months. Tins of beans, vegetables, meat, tuna and milk. She filled the trunk with crates of coca cola, beers. My grandfather helped to carry the groceries inside. Then he locked the car doors, not noticing that Buddy had jumped into the rear.

Later, that hot afternoon, Helena saw Buddy lying sleeping on the back seat. She knocked on the window; she shouted his name. Then she realised Buddy wasn't asleep, he was dead.

"Poor dog," Helena said. "I still remember how Granny cry."

I reminded Helena that by the time my mother, Luke and I arrived for the summer holidays, the curfew had lifted. My grandmother had a new dog. His name was Lucky.

In the half light, I stood before the mango tree. It was full and heavy with fruit. I had almost forgotten what I had come here to do. I started to pick the mangoes from the lower branches and drop them into the bucket. Helena was watching me. She looked sad and old.

"I teach Kenneth to do better; I tell my son treat ladies good. I tell my daughter, don't take no nonsense from no man. Be independent and strong. Don't be like me. But dog cyah make cat."

JOE

The refinery looked strange at night, with its white lights and clouds of puffing silver smoke. Joe once said it looked like the future. "What does Joe know about the future at eleven years old," I'd teased. He didn't say anything. He rode up and onto the verge, where the grass was tall and the road dipped down with the bend. I was trying to keep up, but my breath was short and the muscles in my calves were aching. I said, "What are you having for dinner tonight?"

He slowed down, made a figure eight.

"Roti."

"Is that all?" Loretta had said Joe stopped eating the day Sandra left.

"No. Roti with tomato sauce and a Buster drink."

"You've got to eat more than that you know; there's nothing in flour and water." While I watched him pedalling away down the hill in the dark, I thought, yes, Loretta is right, Joe's all legs and arms, and his head looks too big for his body. I shouted, "You should have lights on that bike!" but he didn't seem to hear me.

It was usually late when Jimmy came home from the Spanish style bar. He staggered into the house, turned off the lights and went straight upstairs to bed. Joe was usually watching television alone in his room or playing games on the computer. Sometimes, if he felt like it, he did his homework or played the phone game. He'd telephone Sandra and hang up when she answered. Then he'd phone again and hang up, over and over, until she took the receiver off the hook.

Sometimes, when I heard him shouting at his father, I thought what's the world coming to, and what if I'd done that when I was a child. *You mother*, he yelled, leaving out the F or the C word. Then he'd slam the screen door, jump on his bike and ride up the hill as fast as he could. Some said, "Poor little boy, what chance has he got with parents like that?" Others were less sympathetic because Joe had done something awful, like killed a cat or peed on their fence or poured cooking oil all over their cars.

Once, when he was angry, he waved a cutlass at Loretta. She used a chair for a shield, backed him into the pantry, then ran out and locked him inside.

"You're nothing but a coolie maid!" he shouted from the window. Loretta sat in the veranda with her face in her hands and cried. She said she never thought white people would get on so.

My mother said it was an awful situation; no matter how you looked at it, the children always suffered the most. She often loaned Joe video films or played cricket with him in the yard. He was in and out of our house like it was his own. Charlie didn't seem to mind. Sometimes she put her hand on Joe's head when she was seeing him out or adjusted the collar of his school shirt. "You can't go looking like that," she'd say, smoothing out the creases with her pretty hands.

I thought she was too soft, and I often told her this. Like the day he borrowed money for a home delivery pizza, and she got upset when I asked him for the four dollars back. She said let him be, he's all right. I said you shouldn't let him get away with these things. What's a little boy like that ordering pizza for anyway?

I remember when she helped him make a model of an Amerindian hut for his history homework. They spent all day fixing the clay, packing it around a plastic bowl, cutting up straw and sticking it on. Then Joe made a tall thin figure carrying a baby, and said it was her. I said, "Who's the baby?" He turned, glaring, and stuck the chisel hard in the workbench. I thought perhaps we shouldn't leave him alone out there.

Joe didn't like me and he made this quite obvious. I understood why and I didn't resent it. Before, while Charlie was at work, he had my mother to himself, and then suddenly I was back home, taking her into town, or helping her in the kitchen, or following her around the yard like he used to do while she watered her plants. One day when she was upstairs, he asked me when I was going back to London. I said, "Never in a million trillion years. I'm sorry, Joe – I'm here to stay."

After that, he seemed to accept me and mostly we got on fine. If I was going to the store in the car, he often came for the ride. I'd buy him a lollipop or a chocolate bar to eat on the way home. And in the evenings, when I went for a run around the refinery camp, Joe sometimes rode alongside or raced ahead and then came back to meet me. I'd say, "Slow down Joe, slow down." And he'd say, "Speed up, turtle, speed up."

Sometimes I teased him, and he'd get annoyed, especially when I made jokes about girls. I'd say, "What about Katie, Joe, she's pretty." And he'd put his fingers in his ears. Or, "Don't you like girls, Joe? One day you'll be kissing them like nobody's business." Then he would throw himself down and crawl around the floor in a way that made me think of an insect, saying stop it, or hitting his head on a cushion. It was quite peculiar, and I couldn't help but laugh even though I knew I shouldn't. If I went too far, he got in a huff and went home.

They say a boy's first love is his mother. I didn't know if that was true, but those days Sandra was hardly ever around. When I asked him questions about her, he'd give me a one-word answer. I knew he loved her, and he wished she'd come home and stay home so things could be like they used to be. Sometimes she turned up out of the blue. She never stayed long, and always left with something: a potted plant; or a tablecloth, a lampshade. Jimmy would stand by the door stuttering and stammering in a loud voice. Then as soon as she'd gone, he'd come straight down the hill to tell my mother what had happened. But my mother couldn't understand very much when he spoke so quickly. Joe said Jimmy talked like a German with bullets in his mouth. As my mother said, "It's just as well that Loretta never went away to America; at least one woman has been constant in his life."

Guavas were in season. All that week, when Joe came home from school, he helped my mother collect them from the ground and the lower branches of the tree and together they filled her big white bucket. Then she carefully peeled them, boiled them with sugar and poured the liquid into jars. She gave the jars of jelly away to friends or put them away in a cupboard. When I lived away, I always took a jar back. Mostly, I left it in the refrigerator, untouched. Now and then I'd take off the lid and sniff it and think about home.

That particular day, I was reading a book when the sweet familiar smell drifted upstairs and floated above my bed. It reminded me of when I was a child in my old aunts' house where there were always pots of the syrupy liquid boiling on the stove. "Don't go near those pots," they'd say and send us outside to play. I thought how things seemed so much easier then. We played kick the can or jacks or cards. Sometimes we picked mangoes and sold them on the side of the road. Or dressed up in costumes and put on shows for the grown-ups. We were in bed by nine, up with the sun and outside playing in the yard before breakfast. These days kids watch too much TV and go to bed too late.

It was after five, so I decided to go downstairs and make some frilly tops for the lids. In the kitchen, there were fifteen small jars of ruby-brown liquid lined up like skittles, cooling on the washstand. When I looked in the sink at the green peel, the seeds, and tiny white worms, I remembered why I never ate them raw. Outside, the light was changing into mint blue and the tall grass was thick and inky green. Under the tree, Joe was jumping up and down in a pile of mahogany leaves making a sound like maracas. "Haven't you got homework to do?" I asked. He looked up, shrugged, and carried on jumping.

I was looking for cloth in the back room when he came inside the kitchen with the big red ball and started bouncing it around the table near the jars of jelly. I wanted to say, please go home and leave me alone, but instead, I went to the sink and found a wriggling worm.

"Joe! Come eat one of these!" He carried on bouncing the ball as if he hadn't heard me. "Joe," I said, "If you don't quit doing that, I'll…" "What?" He looked at me in a challenging way and bounced the ball again. "I'll kiss you. Come on Joe. Kissy, kissy, kissy. Are you scared of girls?" He narrowed his eyes. Then I don't know why but I got carried away. "I bet you like kissing girls really. Katie, Katie. Just pretend I'm Katie." I began to shimmy across the kitchen, jiggling my hips like the big women at Carnival time, to where Joe was standing stiff like a mast, his eyes like two shiny nails.

"Come on Joe, give me a kiss." He started edging towards the door. Like tentacles, my curling hands were inches from his neck. I puckered my lips like a fish.

"Get away!" he screamed. Then, in a high and terrible pitch, "Get away you fucking Bitch! You can kiss my fucking ass!" Joe ran out, slamming the screen door behind him.

My mother came running inside and asked what I'd done to Joe? I said, "Nothing." Then, I told her what had happened. "He can't talk to me like that. Unless he says sorry, I won't speak to him again." She shook her head in a hopeless way and said, "You know what he's like. Let it go."

That night I went to see his father and told him what had

happened; that I wanted an apology. He laughed. "Joe, say sorry? Never."

"But he cursed me."

"Well, he curses me too, but there's nothing I can do."

For days he stayed away. It was quiet without him. I liked it in a way, and I thought Charlie probably liked it too, but I knew my mother was upset. She said it was bad; Joe had no one but his drunken father. I told her not to worry – he'd be back. Sure enough, that same afternoon I saw him riding up and down the driveway making hoops around the frangipani tree.

"You see, what did I tell you?" I said to my mother. "He's not coming in, though. Look, he's riding up the hill."

Another week passed before we saw him again. And if I hadn't gone outside to find my mother and say the clothes were finished and should I put them out, we'd never have known he was there. Joe was hanging around the workbench with a penny cool. When he saw me, he looked embarrassed; then he climbed on his bike and rode away. My mother called out but he didn't look back. She said he must be mad with her too, and what had she ever done to hurt him.

She was glad when we saw him later that day in the store, following his father up the liquor aisle. She went up behind him and tapped his shoulder. He looked happy to see her, especially when she ruffled his fair hair in a playful way. Then he must have asked who she came with because my mother pointed, and he looked towards me. I walked around the corner to the cold storage. On the way home, my mother said she wished I'd speak to him and stop this nonsense. I said he had to learn.

Part of me wanted to say, okay, let's forget it ever happened. But as time went by, I found it harder and harder to give in. And before I knew it those quiet Joe-less days became quiet Joe-less weeks.

I was tying up my laces when I saw his shadow by the screen door. I said, "Funny without Joe about the place isn't it?" I caught my mother's attention and signalled to the door.

"Yes, it's like something's missing." She was chopping a stick of cassava, a white long bone.

"Shame he doesn't come running with me anymore."

"Yes," my mother said.

"All I wanted was an apology. Then everything would have been okay. We used to have such a good time. Joe and me."

"Yes," my mother said again.

"Sorry." It came like a chirp of a small bird.

My mother and I looked at one another.

"What was that?" I said.

"Sorry." It was louder this time.

I looked at the door and then at my mother. Then, without a word, I walked outside, straight past Joe with my head down low so he couldn't see my smile, and I kept on walking and walking up the drive until I reached the frangipani tree where I turned and yelled over my shoulder.

"Are you coming or what?"

He rode alongside me most of the way to the club. Sometimes he took off ahead, then made a loop, and came back to meet me. We didn't speak because there was nothing to say. I could have said, *You're a star Joe, you're a bloody star! I knew you had it in you*. But I didn't. I just kept running and running down the hill like I might never stop while Joe rode away and came back. There were more people out that night – everybody was getting into shape for Carnival. Some were running alone; some were walking, in pairs or groups. My body felt light and tight as I passed a group of young women jogging. The sun had almost gone, and the sky was a perfect purple blue. There were a fistful of stars and one in the white bowl of the moon. A Hindu moon, an auspicious time.

"Joe, do you know what auspicious means?"

But Joe didn't hear me. He was riding down Lime Avenue where the big dog lived. "Don't go down there," I shouted.

In the big field below, the great cotton tree was a tall black lady in a long skirt and the fireflies were a thousand diamonds glittering in the grass. Running on the empty flat by the lake, my hair came loose from its band and blew behind me in the cool wind. How good it felt to be alive. How beautiful Trinidad is, with its lush forests and its pretty mountains and the wild beaches up on the Atlantic side. Thank God I don't live in that awful cold country anymore.

Joe was far in front now, head down, back flat, coming to the bend where the road dips. Approaching the verge, I watched as he rose up in his saddle, let go of the handlebars, and stretched out his arms like Jesus. I called, "Way to go Joe!"

The lights were on full beam, and thinking back now, I couldn't tell if I saw them before, or after I heard the brakes. Then came the loud thock of his body hitting the bonnet, and thock again, when he hit the hood, and smack when he landed on the road. I don't know if I screamed or how I got there so quickly. I can't remember running. It was all whirling and blurred.

She didn't see him. He was going so fast. Did he have lights on the bike? I said it doesn't matter, just get a phone and an ambulance. She asked where he lived. I put my hands in the air – there's no one there. What about his parents, where are they? I don't know. There's a phone at the bar. Then a car pulled up. I didn't know I was crying until a man put his arm around me and said, "Don't cry, love."

There were more than twenty people gathered around when the siren started, and the red lights flashed in the distance. I was on my knees, staring at his face when two men in white jumped out, and one of them checked Joe's pulse. They asked the crowd to move away and lifted him onto a stretcher, covered him up with a baby blue blanket and carried him inside the ambulance.

I climbed into the back before anyone asked who I was. Someone called my name, but I pretended not to hear and said, "Close the doors, somebody."

My mother said Jimmy had come home late that night. He locked the doors and turned off the lights downstairs. When she saw the light go on in his bedroom, she called him on the phone, but he didn't pick up. She rang the bell of the house, over and over; then went back home and let the phone ring until past midnight. She threw stones at his bedroom window until exhaustion came and dragged her home. It wasn't until seven o'clock the following morning, that she saw him drinking coffee by the screen door. He looked at his watch and rolled his eyes when he saw her coming up the hill. "If you're looking for Joe, he's not up yet. Just like his mother, sleep all day, play all night."

Sandra came over to the house the following day. Her face was swollen. She stood in the doorway, and I wondered if my mother was going to invite her in. Afterwards, my mother said that when someone loses a child, you can forgive them anything. Sandra sat down on the verandah chair, put her face in her hands and her whole body shook like we weren't in a hot country, but somewhere very cold and she was naked.

RAY

Every summer, during school holidays, I might see Ray hanging around the house with my cousin and Luke, working on their go-carts or fixing up their skateboards. They were always taking odd bits of metal from somewhere and making them into something you could put an engine in. In later years I would see him up at the beach with a crowd, smoking, listening to loud music, drinking beers from a cooler. Now and again, I ran into Roxy, and I asked about her brother. She knew I had always liked him. They looked alike. When I was older and able to drive my mother's car, I occasionally saw Ray at bars or parties, but most of the time he was away at university. We didn't meet again until one December in the car park of a plaza in Port of Spain where we arranged to hook up at an open-air restaurant.

Here, while a salty, warm breeze blew and the sun disappeared into the sea, we talked about many things. I remember Ray saying that the point about leaving an island is that you have to have something to go to, like school or a job. That's how he got out when he was young. He told me that while he was at university in the USA, he had managed some travelling, so he knew about other places. He knew Europe quite well. I was surprised at how well he knew London. Hearing those names – Portobello, Kensington, Serpentine, Victoria and Albert Museum – felt good that night, sitting by the black water where the boats were anchored, pretty sailing boats with coloured flags from all over the world.

We drank a large jug of cold beer, and he talked for a while about the two women found dead in a house on the outskirts of the city – their bodies so badly beaten, the police could barely tell which was which. He mentioned Roxy and I said how sorry I was, and that Roxy was way too young to die. He said his mother still talked about her as though she was very much alive and living down the road. At that point, I didn't know what to say. I looked away at the moon, thin and white like a fingernail.

I told him about the place I had rented in Ladbroke Grove, with a roof you could stand on and look out at the whole of West London, and he seemed impressed. I told him that I'd lived next door to a famous politician. "You've led a glamorous life," he said, folding a paper napkin into a slim oblong. I wondered if I was giving him the wrong impression. I didn't tell him about Arnaud, or Sam and how unhappy I had been, how Della had to telephone my mother and ask her to send a ticket at once. Later, though, while driving home alone along the dark highway, I thought he'd been right in some ways; my life had been glamorous, at least until now.

Ray usually slept with his body turned to the wall; the white sheet pulled down to his waist. It was very hot in his apartment. Car alarms went off all around the neighbourhood and dogs were always running about and barking at the back; at least it seemed that way to me, though if there had been an air conditioner, we probably wouldn't have heard a thing.

When he first showed me around – the two rooms, small bathroom and tiny kitchen – I said it was pleasant enough and compact, and the rent – only $1500.00 a month – was pretty good for Maraval. There wasn't much furniture – some wooden chairs with large swirly cushions, a 70's style coffee table, and a tall white lamp that had a dimmer switch you had to click three times for low, bright, and off. I liked the shutters; they were the old-fashioned kind I remembered from childhood, that you wound up and could trap your fingers in. On the walls there were carvings of Amerindian weapons – three in a row in pale wood, and on another wall, above the television, were two curved swords with brass handles. "A proper bachelor pad," I said, and laughed. "Look out Port of Spain."

"It will have to do for now," he said, his face very serious.

The thing is, when you checked in the paper under the letting section, you never found anything below $3000.00. Often that was in US$, too, which was an amount, generally, only foreigners could afford – the ones who came to work in oil or construction. Now and then, I reminded Ray, or I reminded myself, that perhaps things weren't so bad as we sometimes made out. I'd do this when he was complaining about the people downstairs or the Christian woman across the hall who liked to park her station wagon in his spot. I'd say, "This is a good deal; don't forget that for one minute."

Sometimes I stood on the little balcony and leaned over and looked down on the narrow street which, after a couple hundred yards, peeled off to a shopping mall where you could pick up groceries or videos. There was a pharmacy, too, and access to the main road that twisted through town. If I peered far right, I could see the back of an apartment complex that always seemed to have a lot of people coming and going at all hours. At night, I could look up to see, through the tall mahogany tree across the road, the amber glow which came from the city, and watch the bright stars. I'd say how lucky he was to have his own veranda, how almost continental. I'd think about the people way up in the hills in tiny wooden houses that were more like shacks – collecting their water in a bucket from a lousy standpipe, and I'd remind him about them too.

Ray said it wasn't good for me to stand there on the balcony – especially in just my T-shirt. This isn't England, he'd say. The people across the road were probably laundering money or selling drugs and wouldn't think twice about coming over here and killing the two of us if they thought we might suspect. One time when he said this, I was pressed against the railings watching a slow-moving blue car with loud music pouring out through the windows, and he was in the kitchen making a cup of coffee.

"Come away from there," he said through the hatch, and I turned around and lifted my T-shirt so he could see that I was naked underneath.

Then, "Come away for Christ's sake." I lifted my T-shirt again, up and down, so the flashing air blew over my hot skin, until he put down his coffee cup and marched across the little room and pulled me inside. Ray said cocaine was big business. Tons of it passed through the docks in Port of Spain and landed up all over the USA.

Behind the apartment, on a road you could take to the sea, there were fancy newly built houses, painted all kinds of pastel colours. This seemed to be a popular trend. But the verandahs were not full of people as they would have been at one time – people talking and drinking and watching the world go by. The verandahs were empty, and the houses looked all locked up, as if no one lived there. There were many houses like this, not just in the capital, but also in pockets of the suburbs. "Why bother with a verandah," I said, one afternoon, when we were coming back from the beach in the Mazda 323 and winding through the end of Santa Cruz where some of those grand houses had started to appear. Sometimes there were fierce-looking armed security guards sitting outside in a purpose-built hut, often with a guard dog like an Alsatian, or a pit bull terrier.

Pit bulls were big business. They often escaped and tore around the place. One day, a pit bull took the face off a young man right outside a supermarket in San Fernando. The dog was chewing up the man's neck, and people were standing around watching, like it was something they had paid to see. No one knew what to do. The dog even ate the man's hair. Eventually, someone had to come with a gun and shoot it. On the news there were big red puddles of blood and the dead dog, right where usually a woman sold lottery tickets. A couple of witnesses were standing by; one of them had her hand over her mouth and she looked like she had been crying. Ray said this place is barbaric.

It all starts with education, Ray said. He had been teaching in a government school in St Anne's. There were never enough books to go around, and the classrooms were shabby and overcrowded – but the job gave him just enough money to cover the rent on his apartment and meet the monthly payments on his car. It was also something he believed in. A good education could make a lot of difference. But the fools running the government of Trinidad and Tobago didn't seem to have a clue about that.

"Trinidad can break your fucking heart," he said, one day, when we were driving back from South Trinidad where I still lived with my mother and Charlie. The cane fields were a green swaying sea on either side of the highway, and the sky was light blue with a single star, which I figured was Venus. I gradually came to know what he meant when he said this. If you go to Trinidad for a vacation, perhaps to see people you know or love, the minute you land you're counting the days before the awful moment when you have to say goodbye. But if you live there, you are always planning how to get out. Sometimes you want to leave simply because things get too much: the heat, the cars, and the way some people look at you. Some people look at you as if they would like to see you dead. Men in particular, like the men I saw sitting on the promenade when I drove by, slowly because either the roads were thick with traffic or they were flooded with brown water, and those men often stared at me like that.

And yet, with all that, there were places Ray took me that

were so beautiful, they must be right up there with some of the most noted beauty spots in the world. Like Chancellor Hill, for instance. You could take a long walk up to the top and look down through the bush and the overgrown vines on the old hotel where Hemingway once stayed. Sometimes, when it rained, steam rose off the hot ground and puffed into small cream clouds. People had built houses there and some seemed to teeter on the edge of the hillside. The gardens of these houses were well manicured, often with bright flowers and unusual coloured shrubs. Some of them came with swimming pools.

One time when I was gazing up at one of them, Ray asked me what I was thinking about. I pointed up at a yellow house that appeared to be almost glowing in the pink light.

"I was thinking about that house and how I'd love to live there."

"If that's what you want," he said, "what are you doing with me?"

Ray could be snippy and unkind. At first, I couldn't understand it, but then I realised it came from his own pain, a disappointment in how his life had turned out. In Trinidad, he said, life is a game, and the one with the most toys wins.

Then there was the refinery camp. Sometimes Ray left school early and we took the long drive up the highway to Charlie's house and walked around the camp, beyond the silver pipes and the shimmering lake with the big, black birds. He'd try and get there before dark; that way we could look for alligators in the lake. If it was already dark, we might take a flashlight and catch their red eyes like bits of fire burning in the blackness. Later, we might go into the Spanish-style bar at the club and drink a cold beer or two. Men sat on the old stools, talking about nothing in particular. Sometimes Charlie was in there, and Jimmy, and we said hi and talked for a while about this and that. I liked the bar with its lime-coloured arches and wrought-iron railings. Above the till, there was a painting on the wall of a girl who looked like Roxy. The girl had a flower in her wavy long hair, and she looked Polynesian and serene.

Now and again, we'd take the route to the tracking station along the smooth road the Americans built during the war, parked the car by the golf club house and made our way through the forest. Then we headed through the bamboo tunnel to a wide, overgrown path that, for a while, followed the sea. Soon the path wound inland and then it started to rise up towards the tracking station. I told Ray that I had been to the tracking station a couple of times with Sandra when I was younger.

Ray said the place wasn't very safe, and if anyone should know he should. Apparently, Roxy used to go there with her friends every weekend, particularly when the moon was full and bright. Sometimes, on a Saturday night, according to people who knew her, Roxy went with twenty or more young people, high on rum and angel dust, piled into cars and roared up the American road to the tracking station.

The walk up was long and lonely, and we never went all the way to the top. I didn't have anything to say about that. It was up to Ray. Sometimes, we only walked to the end of the forest or through the bamboo tunnel and I could see the dish through the trees. Sometimes we walked as far as the silver tree that stood alone.

It was here by the silver tree that Ray first gave me the impression he liked me. We had come through the bamboo and were looking down at the orange and brown rocks and the water rushing around them. The water was very blue on this side of the island, and it wasn't as calm.

I said, 'You've got to grab every moment, haven't you?' and put my hand on a branch. The wind was blowing my hair away from my face.

"Of course." Then he said, "You have something. You're different," and touched my cheek.

I mostly saw Ray on the weekends. Occasionally we might see each other during the week if I borrowed somebody's car, or if I hitched a ride with my mother or if he drove south to see me. Sometimes, I thought a weekend was more than long enough for him.

Little things could set him off. I might mention London, and the flat in Ladbroke Grove, with its large, airy rooms and soft leather furnishings. No matter how many times I told him that the rent was cheap and the flat belonged to a friend, it didn't seem to matter – he seemed to think that I felt the world owed me a living. Or I might talk in a wistful way about my English friends that he said sounded fancy. Sometimes I talked about Sam, until he said I was naive, that I had fallen into a hole. I told him about Arnaud, and how he had vanished from my life. Ray said Arnaud sounded unhinged. I talked about Della too, but he didn't seem to think that Della would like him. If I complained about the heat and the water that was warm when it came out of the tap, Ray said that London water had been through seven people by the time it found its way into your glass. I'd argue that this wasn't true. Hours passed when we didn't speak to one another. I'd gather up my clothes and my toiletries, put them in my weekend bag and wait until he was ready to drive me home.

It wasn't always like that, of course. Little things I did could make a difference. Like when I made a Betty Crocker cake and we ate it straight out of the oven, or when I rubbed cream into his sun-burnt back and blew cool air on his neck; when I turned up at his apartment with a brown bag of cold beers. These things could brighten his mood.

Ray lost his job when the government made cuts in education. His job was one of the first to go. They were sorry to lose him, they said at the school, but there was nothing they could do. When I asked him about it on the telephone that morning, the same morning he had gone into

the school and been given notification, he didn't want to talk
about it. "Don't try and make it alright," he said, irritated.
"There's nothing to say."

I suggested we take a drive somewhere, perhaps to the
open-air restaurant where we could drink a beer, talk, and
look at the sailing boats while the sun was going down. He
didn't want to go and said as much. He would prefer to stay
at home and maybe we could talk later.

That afternoon, I found a ride into Port of Spain with
Sandra who was on her way to the US embassy. Along the
highway, we listened to the radio and talked about her plans
to go away. We also talked about my mother, and Sandra said
she didn't think things would ever be the same between
them. I told her she was probably right, and if it wasn't for
Joe, they might not be speaking. I told her I was sorry.

We got into town quickly. There was a cruise ship in the
docks; a lot of white people were walking towards the main
road. I wondered where they had come from and where they
were going. Soon we were swinging into the car park at the
back of the apartments where Ray lived. Before she drove
away, Sandra said, "Go easy."

When he opened the door, Ray didn't look surprised or
glad.

"Hi," I said enthusiastically. "I've come to cheer you up.
Let's go see the sailing boats."

There was a lot of traffic around the Savannah. The heat
felt damp and thick. For some reason the air conditioner
had stopped working. I leaned over into the back and found
a *National Geographic* magazine which I used to fan myself.
"Don't get it bent up," he said, "I haven't had a chance to
read it yet." Sometimes the heat was unbearable to me. Even
wind blew hot like straight from a fire. If only I could feel
cold for a day, I'd think.

"This place is getting like London," he said; "too many
fucking people."

I looked out of the car window at the people who had stopped to buy soft drinks from a cart under a large poui tree. Its blossom had made a pink carpet. I liked these trees, the way their blossom appeared overnight and then was gone almost as quickly. A fair-skinned man was leaning on a car, drinking Coca Cola and I wondered if he had come from the cruise ship. The flowers gave him an impressive backdrop. He was wearing a black shirt and black trousers and reminded me of someone. Marty St James and the Georgian house in Soho, the bubbles that floated everywhere, and the strange perfume.

Ray said, "Do you know him?"

Without thinking, I said, "In my dreams."

He made a funny, laughing sound. "Would you really like to go and talk to him?"

"Sure."

Next thing, he pulled over to where the man was standing and told me to get out of the car.

I said, "What's going on?"

"You tell me."

"I was only joking," I said.

He turned the car around and took off up the highway. When he dropped me home, I didn't say goodbye. I got out of the car, slammed the door and walked straight inside the house.

I spent the next few days hanging around my mother's place, reading magazines and watching movies. If a car approached the house, I went to the window and looked out through the white net expecting to see the Mazda pulling into the driveway. When the phone rang, I'd tell my mother, "If it's Ray, I'm not here." But he didn't visit our house, and he didn't phone either. I asked Sandra if I should call him, and she said I should make him sweat a little.

When I finally telephoned his apartment, he didn't sound

surprised to hear my voice. He said, "What have we got to talk about?"

"Why are you doing this?" I asked. He said it was time I pulled my head out of the clouds.

"What are you saying? I just want everything to be okay."

"You have no idea," he said.

"You'll find another job."

He hung up.

That night, I lay on my bed and looked at the ceiling where the fan spun like a propeller. I thought how life seemed to come in cycles, how we find ourselves doing the same thing over and over. I remembered other times when I had found myself in similar situations. There were a lot them.

Over the following weeks, I listed these situations in a notebook, chronologically. I poured over their details trying to calculate the exact moment at which each situation began to deteriorate. Sandra said there was nothing to figure out, and I was better off without Ray. As far as she could tell, we were both in a transitory stage of our lives, and we were keeping each other company while we made other plans. After all, she said, you never seemed particularly happy.

Each day, although the sun was bright in the yard, there seemed to be a thin glass panel between the world and me. As weeks passed, this glass panel seemed to grow more opaque. You can wear sadness, I thought, like an item of clothing, a hat or a coat that you can't take off. I thought if only Roxy was here, Roxy with her foresight and chutzpah, she might tell me what to do about her brother.

Occasionally, I borrowed Sandra's car and drove up the highway to Port of Spain where I wandered about the shopping mall. I slowly cruised around the block where Ray lived. Once I parked in the spot below the window of his apartment. I knew he wasn't home; the shutters were closed and the gate was tied with a heavy chain. I drove to the Hill and walked up to the top where I sat on the broken wall and looked down on Hemingway's hotel until it was dark.

Then I heard from someone that Ray had gone away for a month to Miami. He was checking out courses in a foreign university. At last, I accepted that it was over.

★

I didn't usually go to that particular plaza because it was further away from home, and the traffic was terrible with the new works on the highway. But Sandra had told me it was worth checking out the new Brazilian imports in the shoe store, and I knew I would soon be needing proper shoes, not the slippers or sandals I was used to wearing, so I raced through the back roads to get there in time, and was pulling into a spot around the side of the mall when I spotted Ray coming through the double doors. Even though it had only been four months, at first, I wasn't sure if it was him. He was wearing a patterned blue shirt I didn't recognise, with new white jeans. He had lost weight, and his hair was very short.

I couldn't decide whether to drive right past him or stop the car and jump out. Perhaps, you never really have to decide those things, you just find yourself doing them. Before I knew it, I had banged my horn, rolled down the window and shouted something. He had stopped by the bank machine, put his hands up on his waist and glanced around. When he saw me, he stood completely still. Then he started walking slowly towards the car.

"Can you believe this?" I said, leaning out of the window. When we had met – almost two years before – it was in almost the exact same place. I was with my mother; it was Christmas, and the car park was jammed, the stores full with last minute shoppers.

"Serendipity," I said. "How about that? It must be a sign." He put his hand on his chin and smiled. Then I said, "Is this the new Ray?" and he shook his head and looked down.

"Maybe we should talk," I said.

"Sure. If you want. I'd like that."

I parked near the small white golf club house. Ray was leaning against the bonnet of his car, looking towards the track which led to the smooth road. As I walked towards him, I thought he looked happy.

He said, "Lock your door."

"Yes sir!"

Everything appeared a darker green – apart from the shocking red flowers shooting up like flames from the dense bush. Although the air was still, it was cooler, a change in seasons.

"If only it was like this all the time," I said.

"Yes. I know what you mean."

I told him about the rain on the way down and how it fell in one place like a bucket poured out of the sky.

"Yes, it does that sometimes."

I told him about Sandra and her plans to go to America for a while.

"What is she going to do there?"

"This and that; you know Sandra."

The bamboo trees made a green roof and a creaking sound, and there was a loud, repetitive screech which I thought might be a howler monkey. Ray had told me, before we broke up, that these monkeys had been brought over from Venezuela at the turn of the century. I hadn't believed him but had since read that this was true. There were many things I hadn't known about Trinidad until we got together. The forests were full of agouti, armadillos, opossums, and wild pigs. There were even tiger cats. But that was nothing; in Guyana there were jaguars that came in your house and ate food from the table while you slept. When he told me this, I remember shaking my head and laughing, and then pulling him onto the newly made bed where we stayed – only getting up for food or water – for two long, hot days. That was at the very beginning.

The arc of bamboo made me think of a long dark tunnel

you might have to go through when you die. I said, "Are we nearly there yet?"

He turned and half-smiled and I was glad that he was smiling. "Don't start with that already," he said, stopping on the path where, through the leaves, the light had made a yellow and green kaleidoscope. "I'd forgotten how lazy you are."

It wasn't true that I was lazy. Sometimes when I was in the apartment, I hadn't felt like doing too much, but that was only because it was hot. I'd push back the rug and lie on the tiled floor and watch cable television, which he said was a lot of Yankee rubbish.

Something moved in the long grass, and I wondered what it could be.

"I tell you, this is a frightening place," Ray said, his voice rising. "For some reason you never wanted to believe me."

Before, I would have said, lighten up or don't be ridiculous.

On the left, the land made a sudden, steep drop to the ocean and I could see the familiar orange and brown rocks. The silver tree was peeling and underneath there was an orange skin. I picked it up and tore it into small bits, which I then flung over the side.

"Like confetti," I said. Then, "You know that hotel, the one where Hemingway stayed?" He nodded and looked down and he kicked a stone near his shoe. "Well maybe that's something we could do, get the whole thing started again."

"That would be something else, wouldn't it?" He folded his arms and stared out at the faint shape we knew to be the start of South America, as though he was really thinking about it. The back of his neck was damp; I could see the dark hair sticking and curled. There were parrots overhead; they were bright green and shrieking.

"They only have one partner," I said, looking up at them. "Like swans."

He rubbed his eyes and blinked a few times. It was a
familiar habit. Sometimes when we were in the apartment
sitting across from one another, he might blink like that or
put the heels of his hands into his eyes. He turned to the
curve in the road and said, "If we're going to make it up to
the tracking station before dark we had better get moving."

"Are you sure you want to go to there?"

The white abandoned tower was dirty and heavily streaked
with rust; the dish was crooked – tilted in a way I thought it
shouldn't be. I looked at its ugly, irregular shape against the
empty sky and thought if a building can be evil, then perhaps
this one is. Around the broad base, there were cigarette ends
and some glass bottles, and old tin cans, and a broken fan. I
wondered how that had got there and gave it a kick. There
was a lot of graffiti on the inner walls – sprayed in red and
dark blue; these included quotes from the bible I recognised
from Revelations, about the end of the world.

Light poured down through the small, decrepit platforms,
and I was thinking about being young, and how you don't
think about danger, sickness, death. I knew only that Roxy
was drunk and high at the time. "Look at me," she'd yelled,
and run to the edge of the dish, stood on her tiptoes and
dived as if from a high board onto concrete below. Her body
was so broken up they said you could put it in a bucket. I
was thinking about this when suddenly, Ray was there too,
peering up inside the column where the ladder used to be.
I could smell his scent, a familiar aftershave like bay leaves.
We were very close, and I thought about touching his back,
but it didn't seem like the right thing to do. In fact, it all felt
wrong – wrong to be there, wrong to have seen him again
in these circumstances. I was sorry we had come. Anywhere
would have been better than this. I wanted to say something
about Roxy, but I couldn't.

From the doorway, I watched Ray stride across the tall

brown grass. I could see the Atlantic. Then something shifted.

"I'm going away," I said, standing in the open space. The sky was a dirty pink colour.

"What?"

"My father is ill." I put my head down. "I have to go back to England. That's why I was in the mall."

He said, "What?" again.

"Buying shoes for my trip." He stepped towards me and he looked confused.

"It's true," I said.

He took a piece of stray hair caught in my mouth and tucked it away behind my ear just as tears started streaming and falling down my cheeks and over my chin, and before I knew what was going on, I heard myself making a terrible whooping noise like an animal in pain. At first, Ray held me lightly, as if he wasn't quite sure if holding me was the right thing to do, but next thing I was panting like an animal, panting and gasping the cool tropical air and there was nowhere else to go but down into the long grass. Here, on his knees he pulled my head up to his thin chest and bent over my hunched, child shape. We stayed like that for some time, until I thought it might grow dark, and we might never make it back to my mother's car. On the way back down the hill, for the first time in many months, he held my hand.

HELENA

They said her mind was drifting; often days passed when she barely left the house. Then the call came that she'd had a stroke; her sight was affected, her speech had gone. Her daughter said if I wanted to see her, I must come at once.

I took the highway north towards Port of Spain, reminded at once of the lawlessness on the roads. Cars slid from one lane to next without indicating. They'd done away with that, Charlie had said. There were more cars on the road now than ever, foreign used cars were shipped in twice a week. There was talk of a new road system, a highway interchange, like Miami's Overtown expressway, to reduce traffic on the road to San Fernando. For now, late afternoon, it was relatively quiet. I could see the familiar hills, their pointy heads, the deep blue sky beyond.

A crate had fallen and rolled out onto the highway from a truck ahead, stacked with wooden crates held on with ropes. I swerved around it. Then another tumbled off, careered into the carriageway, and then another. Jesus Christ. I checked my mirrors, put on my hazards, and accelerated into the right-hand lane, noticing for the second time that day that the car was losing power. Charlie said I'd need to keep an eye. He would take it into the garage next week. I drove around the truck and hit the horn. Through the window, the driver yelled, "Mudder cunt."

On the left, the Beetham landfill. More than two hundred acres of waste, sinking into the earth and affecting the swamplands. An ecological disaster. These people don't care, my mother said. Above corbeaus were circling. They frightened me, these funeral birds. Smoke poured out from the dump, and it looked grey and white, like ash and filth and death. I thought of how people died here on these roads. Pedestrians ran from the Beetham estate to scavenge for scraps in the dump. Speed and force of collisions were like nothing elsewhere. The front page of the *Trinidad Guardian* often showed photographs of dead bodies, distraught relatives. My mother had stopped noticing; she turned the pages as if it was a Lakeland catalogue.

I clicked on the radio, some news about a pre-carnival party, tickets available in West Mall. Twenty thousand visitors were due to arrive any day. The city glistened in the distance.

I turned off the Beetham, drove over the priority bus route and followed signs to Laventille – a place I'd heard about since I was young. A terrible place. A place of shootings, gangs and homicides. Helena had lived here all her life, with her sister, Ida, and her children, Aisha and Kenneth. When she worked for my grandparents, she spent her weekends and holidays at home. After she retired, my grandmother had kept in touch. She'd sent money, clothes, food, a new television. Gifts for the children. I had never met Aisha or Kenneth. I knew only that Aisha worked as a teacher in a local primary school.

The streets were quiet. I drove up Picton Road; a few cars passed on the hill going down. The light was softer now; thin clouds drifted. A small grocer, a health centre, pale green and smart looking. A garage – Fix it Fast. I could be anywhere in Trinidad; there was nothing unusual here. Some children were playing cricket on a grassy patch where an abandoned car lay on its back. Outside a parlour, men were grouped around cages stacked with birds, pretty, colourful birds. What did they do with the birds? Did they sell them? I slowed down, checked the map, and saw the house was just a couple of streets away.

At the crossroads, a man with cropped dreads stared; his

underpants so low I could see a dark patch of his pubic hair. I
tried to accelerate; the car felt heavy, as if filled with cement.
I felt jittery.

Helena's house was on the right, opposite a small wooden
church. I knew it was hers by the two panels of flowery fabric
I recognised from my mother's kitchen curtains. I parked
alongside a wall of corrugated iron marked with graffiti.
A quote from Ecclesiastes: *Wisdom is better than folly, just as
light is better than darkness.* From the trunk I took out a bag
of groceries. My mother had sent some basic supplies and
a small envelope of cash to help with doctor's fees, meds. I
started up the steps.

"Good afternoon," the woman said. "You find the house!"

Her hair was piled on top of her head.

I asked if it was OK to leave the car there. I told her it had
been giving trouble.

"Sure," she said. "My brother's a mechanic; he could take
a look." Then she said, "Come," and I followed her inside
the small house.

Aisha was immediately familiar, as if I had known her all
my life. She was brown skinned, with deep-set penetrative
eyes. In her mid-fifties, she was striking. Tall, big boned, she
looked strong and capable.

The house was modest, as I'd expected. There was a large
sideboard of varnished wood with brass handles; a television
on a wooden table, green floor tiles; a wooden cross with
a silver Jesus. A bookcase with dictionaries, a few books.
There was a leatherette sofa, two chairs with plastic seat
pads. Towels hung on the veranda railings – wrought iron,
painted red and black. The colours of the national flag.

I looked out and over the balcony. Below, I saw a muddy
yard, three or four other houses, then rooftops, and lower
down, more houses. Eric Williams Towers stood tall in
downtown Port of Spain. Beyond, the Caribbean Sea.

"Prime real estate," Aisha said, "but Laventille will always be a blemish. The time when Obama come, they build a wall so he wouldn't see Beetham as he pass it on his way to the Hyatt."

In the kitchen, tea was laid out on a table and covered with cling film. Aisha had made black tea, sugar cakes, tuna sandwiches, cheese rolls.

"You shouldn't have," I said, and I meant it.

"So British!" She broke into a loud, rolling laugh.

Aisha showed me a framed photograph of Helena and my grandmother outside our family house. Another photograph of Helena with me and Luke standing by the pool – taken during the summer I'd met Anne Sanchez. Then two teenagers standing outside a grand, colonial-looking house.

I took a guess, "You and your brother?"

"Yes, when we were small. We resemble, eh?" Then she said, "Auntie Ida work there all her days. A terrible woman, and them burn down her house in the riots."

"Helena told me about this," I said.

She showed me a framed photograph of a good-looking man with Afro hair. He looked like her, the same deep-set eyes. "Kenneth?"

Aisha had never married. She had a daughter in Florida studying for a degree in Graphic Design. Precious worked part time as a waitress in Hooters.

"Best thing. When she come back, she bound to get a good job. Better still, she married and stay right here."

"Then you might emigrate, too?"

"Who could say. It look as if people only leave here to come back."

Aisha told me that she had lost several children in the school where she worked. Caught in crossfires, or revenge killings. Just yesterday, she visited an apartment belonging to the mother of a little girl she taught. When Aisha entered the lift, it was full of blood.

"Blood all over the floor, blood all over the walls. Buttons, everything. So much of blood." She put up her hands. "These people have nothing, and nobody cares. Life real cheap."

Drapes were half drawn, with just enough light to see without turning on the lamp. A mosquito coil was burning. A standing fan rotated next to Helena's bed where she was propped up, her white hair set in neat corn rows. One eye looked off to the left, the other stared straight ahead, fixed like a marble. Aisha had bathed her mother earlier. I recognised the scent of Limacol.

"Can she understand?"

"Yes," Aisha said, bringing a chair. "She know you here."

She would leave us alone for a few minutes.

I felt awkward. It had been at least four years since I had last seen Helena. And yet, she had always been a part of my life, a witness to the goings on in our family. As a child I had both loved and feared her. Now I took up her hand, and I told her how sorry I was that she was sick. I felt some pressure from her fingers, an acknowledgement, perhaps.

I started to tell Helena things she might want to know, things I might tell her if she wasn't sick. I began talking about my mother, and Charlie, and their recent wedding in San Fernando with just four guests.

Did she know that Joe had died? Sandra had left for America only last week. Luke was working in London. I explained that I was going back to England soon because my father was sick. I wasn't sure what I would do, but it was right to leave. And no, I wasn't getting married, not now and, at this rate, maybe never.

Helena stayed in the same position, and her eyes looked out in the same way. She blinked occasionally, and I wondered if this might be a signal. I was certain that she was listening.

Did she remember Roxy? The girl who fell? Well, I had been dating Roxy's brother. But that was over now, too. Again, I felt her pressure on my hand. I said I was sorry I hadn't visited her before in Laventille. Then I mentioned my grandfather. I said I was sorry for any unkindness he might have shown towards her. He didn't mean it, I said. It was the way he was raised. I asked if she remembered Buddy. The dog who died in the back of the car. What a day that must've been. Thank God for Lucky.

Then something happened. Helena started blinking as if she was looking into a bright, dazzling light. Her body began to twitch, sudden, spasmodic movements.

I said, "Are you okay?" She sucked in a lungful of air; put her hand to her throat. "Helena?" I realised she was struggling to breathe. I got up and went to the door and called out, "Aisha!" Helena started panting and straining her neck. Her body was erect and stiff; her arms were two straight rods. She was hyperventilating. I shouted, "Aisha!"

By the time Aisha ran inside, Helena's chest was making a terrifying, rattling sound.

I moved away to let Aisha tend to her mother. I watched Aisha place a tiny tablet on her tongue, put a glass of water to her lips, and say, "Shush. Mummy. Shush. That's right, that's right." Helena's chest was rising and falling and rising and falling. I wondered if she was going to die, and if she was, then it was my fault.

"Through your nose, you don't remember? Breathe through your nose." Aisha was close to her mother's face, looking at her, holding her. "Breathe in, and hold, and out. Breathe in, and hold, and out." Aisha was counting four, then seven, then eight. Four, seven, eight. Eventually, after several minutes, Helena was calm.

I went to the window and looked out. The yard was full of pink and orange light, the kind of light you might see on religious posters with an inspirational quote. On the telegraph pole, a blue bird was singing. I thought, how can these two things – beauty and terror – exist at the same time?

Aisha was sorry. She shouldn't have left me alone. I

mustn't think that it had anything to do with me. Seizures are typical after a stroke. "Just like tremors after an earthquake."

She asked me to sit with her and Helena. We sat together, the three of us. A triptych. One dying, one in her middle years, one with life ahead of her. The room was still like a chapel.

We heard Kenneth arrive. I realised that I should go. It would soon be dark, and I was worried about the car. I didn't want to drive on the highway in the dark.

Kenneth was taller than I expected. Like his sister, he had a large frame. Strong looking in his dark blue overalls with his sleeves rolled up, he'd come straight from the garage on the hill. He didn't want to shake my hand because his hands were full of oil. Kenneth leaned against the fence smoking a cigarette, and Aisha told him what had happened with Helena. Then she told him about my car. I explained that the car was losing power, and I described the truck and the crates, a lack of acceleration. I mentioned Charlie.

Kenneth wasn't sure, but he'd take a guess it was something to do with the spark plugs. Over time, they get clogged up or worn down. Or it could be the fuel filter.

It was still light, but the sun was setting, and night fell quickly these days.

"Don't worry," Kenneth said, and smiled. "Worry is like paying a debt before you even owing."

Aisha brought beers, and we sat on the steps. She put on the radio, and while Kenneth removed the spark clubs from the engine, we listened to songs from the '80s. We ate tuna sandwiches and cheese rolls.

"See?" he said, holding up a dirty metal screw. "Look yourtrouble."

He carefully cleaned the threads with a small wire brush, then checked the gap between the plug and the electrode, rubbing a little grease on the threads. He tightened each spark plug by hand until it was snug. Then he used a wrench to finish tightening. When he was finished, he closed the bonnet. He started the engine, revved it a little, puffs of smoke flew out of the exhaust.

"It go be OK for now. But if you want, bring it back for a proper check-up when you ready."

He offered to follow me home.

"If you say it's okay, then it's okay."

I hugged Aisha and said goodbye. I thought how strong she was. I promised to return before the end of summer; I wanted to meet Precious.

Kenneth followed me out on Picton Road until I reached the priority bus route. The road to the Beetham highway was clear. I put my foot on the accelerator; the engine was full of power. Driving towards the east, I thought about Aisha and Kenneth. They were good people; they were familiar to me, like family.

I couldn't have known then that Kenneth and Aisha were my flesh and blood. Half-sister and half-brother to my mother. Though, once I knew, and I thought of my grandfather's deep-set penetrative eyes, and his large frame, it was obvious. They were the same.

FATHER

Alone in my mother's house, while she was at the market, I was thinking about the time when I was living in a flat in Ladbroke Grove. Every evening, after dinner, I lit a candle and placed it in a holder shaped like an angel. One night, I woke to the shriek of a smoke alarm. The flames were rising above the angel's wings, and the cream wall was streaked with black ugly marks. I quickly plucked the metal candle case from the angel's feet. But it was so hot I dropped it on the wicker dresser, where silk scarves hung on a hook. The hot wax dripped on my feet, and the carpet. As the flames licked around the edge of the dresser, I thought, Jesus I'm three flights up. I slammed my hand down on the little fire, over and over until the flames were gone. I lay in bed until dawn, with my scorched hand in a bowl of ice. I decided I would never say a word to anyone about that night.

I was filling up the sink with fresh water, thinking how it seemed like a million years ago, and that no matter what Ray said, maybe sometimes you're luckier than you know, when my father, who rarely telephoned, rang and told me he had lung cancer.

He said he hadn't known anything was wrong, until he started with a cough that wouldn't go away. It wasn't like a proper cough, he said, it went on and on for weeks. When someone said, you should see about that, he went to Leeds Infirmary, where a doctor took an x-ray of his chest. It might be okay, the doctor had said. Fingers crossed and all that.

After a long silence, I said, "What does it feel like Dad? Does it hurt?"

He took a moment to answer. Then, "Like a fire," he said in a shaky voice. "A fire, burning all day and all night in your chest."

"Let's hope they can put it out," I said, startled by my choice of words.

"Yes, love. Let's hope they can put it out."

When he knew he was dying, my father telephoned more often. I'd take the phone outside and watch the black sky through the trees, while he talked for a long time about nothing in particular. "But how are you feeling?" I'd eventually ask, trying not to sound impatient.

"I'm all right," he'd say in a defensive way. Then he would tell me how he spent all day lying on the sofa, watching television.

Sometimes when he talked about his young son, who didn't know a thing, now living at his maternal grandmother's house, he cried. I wanted to say, *Don't cry, Dad. It will be okay*. But I didn't, because I wasn't sure it was true. Now and again, he'd stop talking and I'd hear a match strike. "You're not smoking, are you, Dad?" He'd say yes and why not? It doesn't matter now, anyway. And I'd think, yes, maybe it doesn't.

When I put down the phone, I'd wander in the yard and look for the moon or a cluster of stars. And I'd think about the cancer, the tumour closing around his heart like a white fist.

As I made my travel arrangements, my mother said she wished I didn't have to go through all this. I told her you couldn't run away from these things. "He is my father after all. If it were you, I would do the same thing."

On the way to the airport, I photographed the land in

my mind: images of coconut trees, the bright blue sky, the
pointed, pretty hills, silver fish hanging by the side of the
road, a truck full of oranges, a burning cane field. I studied
my mother's profile, and her brown hands on the wheel.
One day, I thought, when things are really bad, I can
remember these things.

My father was not there when I arrived, but the woman
upstairs said he was expected back soon. We were in the
garden where the roses were pink and fat, and there was a
pine tree with a strange, distorted shape. By the gate, there
was a crowd of tall purple flowers. The woman said they
were hollyhocks, and that there were foxes in the bushes.
She'd seen two on the rim of the lawn only last week.

She said she often saw my father coming and going from
the house with his stick, and his back all bent and low. She
warned me how much he'd changed, grown thin with big
staring eyes. I wanted to say that he could not look like that,
but when he came from the taxi, trying to see if the woman
approaching was his daughter, I thought, *Christ it's a fact. He
has a a bruise on his cheek and eyes that stare like a fish.*

"He's got worse in the last two weeks," the woman had
said. "Good job you came when you did." She ran her
fingers through her fine straight hair and watched me roll
a pinecone in my palms. There were more around the base
of the tree.

I said, "When I was a child, I collected cones; I sprayed
them silver and gold and put them under the Christmas
tree." The woman smiled in an awkward way.

"Do you think he will last until Christmas?"

She looked up at the summer sky. "You never know with
these things. You just never know."

I wore shoes in the apartment because the floor was dirty
and cold. Newspapers were stacked high in the small

kitchen, among empty bottles, tins of soup and plastic containers of medication. On the large table in the large blue room where he sat all day, there was a wide untidy pile of papers beside my father's chair. I found letters, postcards, empty envelopes, cigarette papers, brochures from banks – and photographs I had never seen before. In one, I was four and holding up a cake in the big house. Alan was standing in the window. My father said he couldn't be bothered with cleaning. A girl came once a week, and she didn't do much except push the broom about.

Beneath the table were unpacked boxes, there since the move at the beginning of the year. He said, "Leave those, love. I'll sort them when you're gone."

Inside one box there were familiar framed paintings: a red fish, a Klee print, a Japanese lady, a plate made of brass, another made of china with a pretty pattern. I took them out and found places for them. The china plate looked nice above the fireplace. The water-colours of plants in wooden frames brightened the hallway. The Japanese lady fitted perfectly above the bookcase. I left the bamboo blind alone.

"What do you think?" I asked, when the pictures were up and the table was cleared.

"Yes, love, very good. Very good."

That evening, we took a taxi through the back streets and up the hill to where my father's mother-in-law lived in a red apartment building with an excellent view of the city. His young son was lucky to live there, I thought. There were shops close by and young people around; there was a feeling of movement. I liked the old apple trees in the garden.

My half-brother didn't look like my father, though he had his figure: the same narrow torso and long legs. There was no trace of a Yorkshire accent when he said, "How do you do" and shook my hand. His eyes were clear and light blue. His elfin face had hardly changed since last we met, five years before.

"Look at you, all grown up," I said. "Can't I have a kiss as well as a handshake?"

"I don't think so." He looked surprised and embarrassed and ran into the house.

My father looked annoyed. He shouted, "Come back! She's come a long way to see you."

The boy's grandmother was a small lady with grey hair and dark eyes. She had a kind face and a strong clear speaking voice. While my father slowly made his way up the stairs, she prepared tea for everyone in her tiny kitchen. In the hallway, I admired her fine ink prints and told her they reminded me of William Blake drawings.

I wanted to ask her about my father, but the boy was in the next room. He must have known something was wrong by the way our father coughed and because of his obvious weight loss. Only six months before, he had taken the boy to school on the handlebars of his bicycle. I wondered why my father hadn't told him. Surely, it would have made things easier.

The boy's grandmother put the teapot on the table, asked if I took sugar and milk. Then, the strangest thing. In her face I saw the face of her dead daughter, Ellen, my little brother's mother: saw her sloping, dark eyes and her turned-up nose and thin mouth. I realised why my father could not tell his ten-year-old son he was dying. It was six years since his mother had died. She died of cancer. She was thirty-five.

That day, while sorting through his writing bureau, I found an envelope of forgotten photographs taken in a town on the west coast of Ireland some years ago. Ellen was all red-faced, braced against the wind, and in her arms, a colourful blanket was wrapped around their son. My half-brother must have been just a few weeks old. Ellen's black hair was pinned at the nape of her neck. She was wearing a flowery dress and sandals. She looked like herself, big and shy and awkward. I remember my father telling me how thin she was at the end. By then the cancer was everywhere.

"She looks nice in this one, Dad," I said.

He stared at the photograph for a long time. Then, he propped it up on the desk by the phone. There were other photographs of my half-brother, taken at different times. He was standing on a yellow beach, hands raised to the sky; little and lying on a grassy bank; licking a big ice cream and leaning on a fence where a girl I couldn't recognise was laughing.

They visited Sligo every year for the summer holidays and stayed in the chalet by the sea. I remember Ellen complaining once, saying she wished they could go to France or Italy for a change. I had often wondered if my half-brother felt the same way. Now his mother was dead, he would have had no choice but to go.

"Does he like Ireland, Dad?" I asked in a tactful way.

My father said, "He loves it. The first time he saw the Irish Sea, he was so excited he ran full speed into the water with all his clothes on."

Over supper, my father and I talked about going back to Ireland. But though I knew he wanted to go, the new weakness in his left side made him unsure about travelling. I noticed how long he took to walk to the door when the neighbour came with a chamber pot. And later, when I asked if he could make the flight, he looked afraid. I said we could get a wheelchair, and who cares what anyone thinks.

He said, "Wait until the morning, love. Wait until the morning. See how I feel then." Then, "If I can't go and everything is worse, I want you to go. Do you hear me? I want you to go with the boy."

It didn't stop raining from the moment we arrived. The sea was grey and flat, and the wind flung the rain across the glass of the double doors that led onto the large terrace.

It was strange to think the old chalet had gone and, in its place, my uncle had built this large and comfortable house. He was humming a familiar tune and looking through the newspaper. His wife was clearing the table from lunch.

She said the weather was unusual for this time of year. Up until last week there was plenty of sun. I said I didn't mind; I'd been living in the sun for more than three years; there were times when the heat was unbearable. Downstairs, the boy was watching television.

Later, when she suggested a drive to the foot of the mountain, the boy didn't want to go.

"Why stick inside the house?" she said. "Come for the drive. We can go to the beach too. And we'll take the dog."

I said, "You know what you'll get if you don't come!" I made loud kissing sounds. He screamed and ran outside, and I thought of Joe.

I noticed how green everything was. The trees were full. And the hedges were thick and tall. Soon they would be full of berries. The cattle were fat and pretty on the sloping field ahead, so different from the skeletal cows in Trinidad – usually tied to trees or bushes. Sometimes, the ropes came undone, and they'd wander away. Once, a plane I was on couldn't take off because a whole herd were on the runway. It was then my mother said, "What madness made me come back to this third world place?"

Eventually, we came to a turning where the land became a huge and sprawling shape.

"God, it looks like a sleeping animal." I wrapped my scarf around my neck.

"Yes," my uncle's wife said. "Let's walk along its back."

The wind was blowing hard, kicking up the sand below and pressing down the tall beige grass. We walked in silence down the stone steps to where the beach began, and water sloshed around large coppery rocks. In the distance, a peninsula made a brown tail and a pointed hill an ear. The sky was diamond clear: a round blue roof.

Soon the dog was racing along the beach in loops, chasing circling gulls and a stick the boy tossed now and then near the sea edge. Suddenly there were children running from the other side, wearing brightly coloured bathing suits.

I told my aunt how I had come here, too, when I was a child – with my mother and father and Luke. We played for hours by the sand dunes. Sometimes my mother read or took photographs or made movies with her special camera. When we were older, we'd put up a screen in the big house and watch them. I told my aunt about Alan and how kind he had been. My aunt said she had heard so. She also heard he'd died a few years ago. I said, yes, that was true.

On the way home, we stopped off at the church. It was not as I remembered, but the gravestone was exactly as before. The boy read the inscription aloud. "Cast a cold eye on life, on death. Horseman, pass by!" He looked confused, then sad.

I said, "Are you missing Dad?"

He said, "Yes" and looked up at the grey sky. "He brought me here last time."

I felt my eyes begin to sting and water. I said, "Don't worry. We can phone him when we get back. He's best in the hospital, you know. The nurses will take care of him."

On the way back to the car, he let me take his hand.

Back in Leeds, as soon as I'd collected my luggage, I took a taxi straight to the hospital where my father's doctor wanted to see me. In a private room away from the ward, the small man with grey hair and kind eyes sat opposite me. In a grave voice, he said he was sorry.

"The cancer has spread to the brain. It's probably only a matter of weeks."

I said I didn't know that about cancer: that a chunk can

break from the tumour and travel away in the blood, that it can root and grow in another place like a plant.

He said sort of, and that was why my father had lost the feeling in his left side, and why he was having trouble with the right. It was why he had swellings and epileptic fits in the night. The doctor said, as soon as he was able, they would move my father to the nearby hospice, the same hospice where his wife died. Before I left, he gently pressed my arm and said again he was sorry.

I was surprised by how much my father had changed in a few days. His feet were all puffed up, so puffed up he couldn't wear the slippers I'd brought. His left arm was also enlarged, and inflamed, and propped on a pillow. His eyes were tired. And for the first time, I noticed they didn't light up when I said, "Hi Dad!" and kissed his cheek.

When dinner arrived, though he was having difficulty holding his cutlery, he didn't want me to help him. The soup dripped on the napkin, and the meaty sauce dropped on his beard and stuck. He drank tea from a special plastic beaker like those that babies use. After ice cream, he was, surprisingly, still hungry. So I broke chocolate into cubes and fed them into his mouth in a playful way. In a flat voice he said, "Thank you, pet."

Then the friendly nurse came in and said, "Time for your pills." She placed them on the table in a little line. When he couldn't manage to pick them up, she said, "Never mind. Open wide," and dropped the tablets onto his tongue. I could tell he was angry. He was glaring at his useless hand.

All weekend, alone in my father's flat, memories came to the front of my mind like watery images from an old and familiar film. The sun coming through the tall windows made strange shapes on the wooden floor. The blue of the room seemed cold and religious.

I tried to keep busy with chores. I washed clothes and pegged them outside on the line and when they were dry, I washed more. I dusted everywhere. I sorted through drawers and cupboards full of papers and documents. I found more photographs. My father was young in some: a tall, fine-boned man with large eyes, and short fair hair.

After my mother left, he left his hair long, grew a beard, and swapped his smart suits for jeans and casual shirts; he exchanged his car for a bicycle, and wore a black knitted hat like a fisherman's cap, which he never took off, even in the summer.

When I was living in the big house, and he came to visit, I'd say, "Dad, please take your hat off." And, "Dad, why do you wear a hat? Do you sleep in it too?" Usually, he'd smile and shake his head, as if I was being ridiculous.

Sometimes, I'd ask, "Dad, will you trim your beard? Please cut it a little." I didn't say I was embarrassed in front of my friends because he looked like a hippie, and why couldn't he be like other dads. Dads who drove cars and wore suits and worked in normal jobs.

I told my friends in the village that he was a distant relative, and no, I didn't have a clue where he lived. I remember watching him walk down the road in his steel-capped boots with his newspaper sticking out from his back pocket and feeling guilty and regretful. But I couldn't help it.

I found some photographs taken in the eighties. He was standing in a misty place. His beard was red like the red autumn leaves on the nearby trees. He looked lonely and distant.

When a nurse from the hospital rang and said my father had gone into a coma, I immediately telephoned my uncle in Ireland. He told me not to worry, and yes, of course he would come at once, on the next available flight. Then I telephoned Luke, but Luke wasn't there.

My father's body was turned to the right, towards the large window where the sun was hidden by clouds. He was breathing into a plastic bag as big as a big lung. Now and then, his hands twitched beneath the sheet in an uncontrolled way and his chest made a terrible rumbling sound.

The nurse said, "When the fitting starts, we have to hold him down."

★

In the centre of the city, my uncle and I had lunch in a pub and talked about other things, like holidays and movies and living in Trinidad. I talked about the beautiful hills behind my mother's house, the coconut trees on my favourite white beach; about the colour of the sea and how different it can be on the Atlantic side. I told my uncle about the market, and the pool where I swam every day; about the heavy rain in the wet season, how it sounded like horses galloping on the galvanised roof. I talked about the dry season, and the fires. I told him about Ray. Then I mentioned breadfruit, mangoes, sweet, sweet oranges, sapodillas, shark and bake, my pretty mother... We also talked about Luke and the fact that he did not want to be a part of my father's life anymore. Luke couldn't understand or forgive our father's behaviour from when we were children. He used to blame Alan, but now he was older, he could see his father more clearly.

My uncle said, "That's sad. That's very sad."

Later, while I was getting ready for bed, my uncle telephoned a taxi to take him to the hospital. He said he didn't want his brother to die alone.

"But how do you know he will die tonight?"

"I do. I just do." His voice was calm and sure. "See you in the morning, love. Sleep well."

In the Chapel of Rest, my father was laid out in a softly lit room on a long table. He was covered with a royal blue cloth,

embroidered with a gold cross. His hair was swept back
from his pale face. Without the knitted hat, his forehead was
round and large, and his features were more pronounced.
His white lips were closed. His beard had been cut short.

While I watched the passing images of stores, trees, houses,
people lit by the bright morning sun, my uncle held my
cold hand steady. I felt as though I had been unfastened,
plucked by the root and hurled to an unfamiliar place. And
yet, strangely enough, in this new place I felt assembled and
concentrated, as though I were bare and somehow essential,
like myself.

I thought about my mother. It was still too early to phone
her. Before I left Trinidad, I'd asked my father if there was
anything he wanted me to bring. I thought he might say
guava jam, or pepper sauce, or a bottle of rum.

"Yes love," he said. "Bring your mother."

When I told her, she looked up from the kitchen sink, all
surprised and pleased. Then she looked distressed. "I can't
believe this has happened to him," she said, with tears in her
eyes.

Then we talked about my theory that people die around
the time of their birthday. I remember thinking my father
would prove it wrong because his birthday was just around
the corner, in July. I had no idea that, even then, there was
a crowd of cancers growing in my father's head, that before
the end of the summer he would be dead.

There were ten years between them. She met him when she
was fifteen while hitching a lift from Dublin to Sligo with
her best friend. My father and his pal picked them up. His
pal married my mother's friend. And as soon as my mother
was eighteen, she and my father were married. In the photos
they looked very happy.

When she phoned that week, she said, "I hope your

theory's wrong. He'll be sixty-four on Tuesday." In the shop I had looked for a suitable cake I could take in for him and the nurses.

Suddenly, I remembered the bags at the hospital. Earlier, on the ward, I had seen his black haversack, the same one I'd packed when he went in, leaning with his stick against the door of the empty room. There were other bags, too: hospital plastic bags with his name on. I told the nurse I would come back for them later. Perhaps I should have taken them then.

"Don't worry, love," my uncle said. "One thing at a time. Let's handle the funeral arrangements first."

I wondered if my half-brother was going to come back from Ireland for the funeral. The social worker said he was old enough to decide for himself. "If he doesn't go," she said, "perhaps he could write a goodbye letter to his daddy, and you can put it in the grave with the coffin." I said, yes, of course.

In a flat voice, with a heavy Yorkshire accent, the funeral director asked if I would like hygienic treatment on my father's body. I wasn't sure what that meant, but I didn't like the thought of my father unclean, so I said yes. The prices of coffins started at four hundred pounds. Satin lining came in white, egg-white, cream, oyster, blue, yellow, pink or light green. Flowers were cheaper when seasonal. There were single sprays or bouquets crossed or placed in a fan. I could order a special wreath in big letters: DAD or LOVE or PEACE. We could hire a choir or select two four-minute tunes from a favourite CD. In the newspaper announcement, I could call my father dear, dearest, special, loving, beloved. My uncle could describe his brother in the same way. When we both picked "dear", the funeral director shook his head. "You can't have two dears," he said. "One of you will have to pick something else." My uncle said it didn't matter, and brother was just fine. Then he gave his address for the invoice.

On the way out, the funeral director said he would let

us know when my father arrived. "Probably not until tomorrow." They were closing up now; it was his half-day.

Outside, the midday sun was warm, and the air was still and thick. The street was busy with lunchtime shoppers. When I was at college, I used to visit friends in this part of the city. It was never like this. Now there were more shops: second-hand shops with impressive window displays, wine stores, restaurants, banks. There was a new large supermarket, where, when I arrived, my father sent me to buy vodka and tobacco and anything I might need. By then he was drinking a bottle of vodka every day.

At first, I was shocked and said, "Dad! Do you have to drink that much?" Then I realised it didn't make him drunk at all.

When I told her, my mother said, "Well, if the cancer doesn't kill him, cirrhosis will."

I told her a bottle for him was like a glass of white wine with a meal for me. In the hospital I took him half-bottles. They were easier to hide.

My uncle and I took a while before we found the Royal Oak, the pub where my father took Luke and me when we were young. It was different now, with a beer garden and a 3 star restaurant. I didn't want to sit outside with a crowd of young people, talking and laughing loudly; so, we sat in a long cool room where there was a television, and bar snacks were displayed in a bright, heated cabinet. I ordered sandwiches and drinks and asked the barman to turn down the volume of the television. I felt very tired and cold. I put my head on my uncle's shoulder and closed my eyes.

The earth was piled high in a small hill and covered with a large plastic sheet. The bearers lifted the coffin up and across, then quickly lowered it down into the brown mouth of the grave. The mother of my father's dead wife had said my father's name could go on her daughter's headstone. I had never seen it before. It was handsome with an old-fashioned look. "Ellen Virginia Griffiths – born June 10, 1955, died June 15, 1992."

After the priest said the blessing, my uncle stepped forward from the small crowd of gatherers. In a small voice, he said, "Thank you all for coming. On behalf of the family, thank you." He held up my father's knitted hat and a small white envelope, then dropped them into the grave.

I didn't know what to do with the books, so I called a nearby second-hand bookstore. When the driver arrived with a white van and a stack of empty boxes, I asked if he took other things, like kitchen utensils and small furniture. "Yes," he said, "everything but refrigerators, stoves and washing machines."

While Luke, who had come for the funeral, sorted through kitchen cupboards and the driver packed boxes, I emptied drawers, and cleared shelves and cupboards. I took down all the pictures and put them at the far end of the blue room, with side tables, old fold-up chairs, lamps, vases, records, and ornaments. I rolled up rugs into long tubes; made curtains into slim oblongs and put them into suitcases with sheets and pillows. Then Luke and I passed everything to the driver through the window. By noon the apartment was almost empty.

"Do you want the television?" I asked. The driver nodded and looked pleased.

"It's on wheels, so we can push it out."

The van was full when I remembered my father's bicycle. It was leaning against the door of his bedroom. The silver blue frame was dusty and there was mud on the wheels, his clips on the handlebar.

Every day, he used to take my half-brother to school on the bike. On the way they sang songs or whistled. "Even in the winter, Dad?" "Yes, pet. Even in the winter." I imagined him freewheeling down the hill, his son sitting on the handlebars, stretching out his arms, grinning in the wind.

One day, when I was visiting him in hospital, I asked if I could borrow it. "Of course you can." Then he paused and looked around the ward. "No, love. Better not. We don't want both of us in here, do we."

"What about the bike?" The driver was behind me. His face was flushed and shiny like a pink moon.

Back in London, the crowds and the lights seemed to belong to a peculiar republic. Black cabs were everywhere collecting and emptying. Open-topped buses were full. People were hurrying underground and rising from below; pouring out onto crammed sidewalks, filtering into stores, theatres, and bars. By the time I reached the apartment, I was exhausted.

That night, I dreamt of Trinidad. I drove around the Savannah in a hearse, and then to my mother's house, where I lay in the yard beneath a samaan tree and watched the burning sky through its black branches, fine like a dome of net. Ray lay beside me for a while. We listened to my mother sing as she washed my city clothes in the outside sink. The water made a dirty river and a dark sea.

I woke to the sound of a garbage truck reversing and making a terrible noise on the street outside the apartment window. I could hear a radio playing BBC World Service. Someone shouted from across the road in a language I didn't recognise. Later, Luke said it's Kurdish, and you should hear them when they get going on a Sunday afternoon.

I spent the following days seeing friends. Over lunches and dinners, I talked about my father, and the kind nurses in the hospital. I told them how I'd packed up the house and given everything away to Oxfam. They said nice things, like: *At least he didn't suffer*, *Good job you came when you did*, and *How well you've coped*. Mostly, I felt okay. I telephoned Ann Sanchez, and she said how sorry she was, and I knew from her voice that she meant it. I remembered how she had been that day at the pool, just after her father died, pretending everything was all right when it wasn't at all.

At the weekend, I went shopping in the high street and tried on clothes in the summer sales. I bought some make up and special shampoo and a pair of canvas shoes I could wear anywhere. Then Della asked me to join her on a trip to see the eclipse. I hadn't seen Della for a long time.

"Come on. An eclipse like this will never happen again. There'll be a group of us. You should take some time out."

I said maybe that I'd give her an answer tomorrow.

That evening, my uncle phoned me to tell me a special mass had been arranged in the town where my father was born. He said I should be there; it was going to be different. "The band is going to play," he said. "You've never heard your father's band."

I didn't want to go back to Ireland. I'd had enough.

"I can't," I said weakly. "I'm going to be away, in Cornwall. Della and me are going to see the eclipse"

"When are you back?" He sounded disappointed.

"Thursday, I think."

"You can get a flight on Friday morning." There was a pause. Then, "You should be here, you know. I want you to read from the Bible."

I remembered the last time I'd read at a funeral. I hadn't known how upset I felt until I heard my own voice. Once I started crying, I couldn't stop. The congregation became a rising sea. I stumbled over words like big rocks. I thought it would never end. Afterwards, on the steps of the church, people I barely knew came and said *Hello*, *how well you read*, and *What a beautiful eulogy*. I remember thinking, never again, not in a million trillion years.

But this was different. I already knew how I felt about my father's death. Every time I thought of him, I was shocked, all over again. Something known had gone, like no more trees or grass or wind. Sometimes I was okay, and then I'd hear a song or look at a billboard, and I would remember him lying twisted in the hospital bed breathing into a clear bag, the bruise like a plum on his face, his swollen feet in hospital socks. In a way, I wasn't really remembering, because it wasn't an effort to recall those images. They were there beneath a thin skin of present sound and daylight.

"I'll think about it." I promised to phone from the country.

"You should see it through to the end." My uncle's voice was unusually firm. "Once this is over, that's it. The last stop on the train."

Della and I set off early from Baker Street and headed out towards the West Country on the endless grey strip of the motorway. The young woman beside me had a theatrical voice.

"I'm so excited," she said. I asked her why.

"The eclipse is going to be amazing! The sky will turn black and the birds will stop singing, and flowers will wilt. The wind will get cold like in winter." Then she told me about her television job; sometimes she was in Italy, sometimes in London. She was buying an apartment in a trendy part of the city. She couldn't wait to move in. When it was her turn to drive, she turned the music up and sang in a loud voice for a long time.

Della said, "Don't cry," when she saw my wet face turned to the window. "You'll be okay."

It took a long time to climb to the top of the ancient hill where there was a ring, a pagan site. There were pretty summer flowers everywhere: purple and frail yellow flowers with long stems. Some walked up the hill with dogs on leads; some carried babies and young children. There was a flock of old women climbing slowly, and a camera crew the young woman knew. At the top, people were spread out around the edge of the huge ring. Some were looking up at the cloudy sky where the sun and moon were each half a disc: a gold and black penny.

At first it seemed to happen slowly. There was a gradual softening of light like a storm was coming. Then everything became darker and darker. And the air was noticeably cooler. Della's eyes were wide. "Oh my God!" Then softly, "God."

Everyone fell silent. There was darkness everywhere, but at the horizon where the moors were, I saw a bright line of daylight. Someone said, "There are horses running in the field below!" But I never saw them or heard their hooves. My heart was beating quickly. I wondered what would happen if the whole world stayed dark. Then it began to grow lighter and lighter. And soon, everything was as it had been.

After, everyone walked back to the farm where lunch was being prepared. The flames were orange and high in the make-do barbecue barrel. New people arrived with friends of friends and said how they wished it wasn't all over so quickly. They found seats beneath the trees where there were salads, bread, and wine arranged on trestle tables. There was plenty of meat to go around. Some people even had seconds.

"Are you okay?" Della asked when she found me wandering by the pond, looking at the hydrangeas.

"I'm fine," I said. And I thought I was, until she put her arm on my shoulder and looked at me in a tender way.

"It just doesn't seem to get any easier." My voice was choked and childlike.

"What can you expect? It's only been a week. Come and be with people. It's important. You shouldn't be on your own."

Soon it was dark, and everyone was dancing in the little room where there was a bar. There was a silver disco ball in a high place and a flashing blue light on the wall. The girl who worked in television jumped around and moved her arms about like a bad swimmer. "Louder! Louder! Turn up the music!" She jiggled her hips and flung her head this way and that.

Then a man I'd spoken to briefly on the hillside leaned over and said, "Come on. Relaaaax!" He passed me a joint. I smiled and raised my glass.

"No thanks. Wine is fine for me." My voice surprised me. It sounded so cheerful.

Outside, the sky was very dark. And the stars, though few, seemed sharp and far away.

★

Flying over the lumpy green land, I thought how strange it looked. There were lakes in wobbly shapes and narrow roads snaking here and there. I could see tiny cows and cars and little houses. Then the clouds were thick, and I couldn't see anything but their pale grey mass.

In the airline magazine there were pictures of a tropical place. I skipped through the article and read about exotic foods, white beaches, fabulous sunsets. I thought about my mother and wondered what she was doing. Today was market day, so she was probably in town. Suddenly, I felt very tired. We hadn't arrived back in London from Cornwall until three in the morning. I wondered if there was time to sleep before the service.

I didn't bother to change. My uncle's wife said I looked fine in my long grey dress and cream knitted sweater. She'd prepared sandwiches and salads and made a big sponge cake. She said they would all come back home, and later, perhaps we could go to the pub.

"How many are coming?"

"You never know with these things. Quite a few, I guess. Your father knew a lot of people, you know."

The band began to play as people entered the hexagonal

church. My uncle and his wife and I stood near the door and met them as they entered. She introduced me as Christopher's daughter, and they said, "Oh, I'm so sorry about your father." They shook my hand and looked into my eyes in a way that said they meant it.

At first, there were two or three people arriving every few minutes. When they found their seats, I asked my uncle's wife who they were. She told me where they lived or how they knew my father.

Then, there seemed to be an endless line of people, and a growing crowd at the door. I shook hands, nodded, and greeted the next one. Some had tears in their eyes. "I knew your father well. What a lovely man." "He will be missed." "I'm so sorry for you." "Your dad was very dear to me." And so it went on for what seemed like a long time, until the church was full, and the priest and bishop were waiting by the altar for people to find their seats. It took so long the band played another song.

I hadn't realised how much I liked traditional jazz. The easy beat of the drum, the soft, leaning guitar, the trumpet mixed with the bass and sweet clarinet, together made a delicious, lazy and soulful sound that reminded me of old movies and smoky bars. On the front pew, I let my shoulders gently swing, and softly tapped my feet. When I looked over at my uncle, he was smiling, and I realised I was too. So, I thought, this is the music my father once played! A sudden heat, like a flame of happiness rose inside and merged with a terrific sadness. I'll never feel like this again, I thought. Never.

After the sermon, I took my place on the stand and read from Corinthians in a loud and clear voice.

ABOUT THE AUTHOR

Amanda Smyth is Irish-Trinidadian and was born in Ireland. She is the author of *Black Rock* (2009), *A Kind of Eden* (2013) and *Fortune* (2020). She has won the Prix du Premier Roman prize, was nominated for an NAACP award, shortlisted for the McKitterick Prize and the Walter Scott Prize for Historical Fiction, and selected as an Oprah Winfrey Summer Read. Amanda teaches creative writing at Arvon, Skyros in Greece, and at Coventry University. She lives in Leamington Spa with her family.

ALSO AVAILABLE

Fortune
ISBN: 9781845235192; pp. 272; pub 2021; £9.99

Eddie Wade has recently returned from the US oilfields. He is determined to sink his own well and make his fortune in the 1920s Trinidad oil-rush. His sights are set on Sonny Chatterjee's failing cocoa estate, Kushi, where the ground is so full of oil you can put a stick in the ground and see it bubble up. When a fortuitous meeting with businessman Tito Fernandez brings Eddie the investor he desperately needs, the three men enter into a partnership. A friendship between Tito and Eddie begins that will change their lives forever, not least when the oil starts gushing. But their partnership also brings Eddie into contact with Ada, Tito's beautiful wife, and as much as they try, they cannot avoid the attraction they feel for each other.

Fortune, based on true events, catches Trinidad at a moment of historical change whose consequences reverberate down to present concerns with climate change and environmental destruction. As a story of love and ambition, its focus is on individuals so enmeshed in their desires that they blindly enter the territory of classic Greek tragedy where actions always have consequences.

'Magnificently absorbing' *The Guardian*
'Don't even read the synopsis, dive right in; *Fortune* is a read that rustles, breathes, takes you by its sultry hand and doesn't let you go.' D.B.C. Pierre